ENCOUNTERING AN EXTERMINATOR
DRAGON WILL BE ONE OF THE MOST
TERRIFYING EXPERIENCES OF HICCUP
HORRENDOUS HADDOCK THE THIRD'S
ADVENTUROUS LIFE.

But hang on. WHY is he meeting
such a deadly creature?

Because over on Lava-Lout Island, which
is FULL of EXTERMINATOR DRAGONS,
the volcano is ready to blow. Now the unlikely Hero
Hiccup faces a Quest to Stop the Volcano
Exploding, alongside his best friend Fishlegs
and Humungously Hotshot the ex-Hero.
Except it's not only gigantic dragons and volcanoes
that await. Hiccup's ARCH ENEMY is also
lurking – and he's seeking REVENGE!

You don't **HAVE** to read the Hiccup books in order.
But if you want to, this is the right order:

1. How to train your Dragon
2. How to be a Pirate
3. How to speak Dragonese
4. How to Cheat a Dragon's Curse
5. How to Twist a Dragon's Tale
6. A Hero's Guide to Deadly Dragons
7. How to Ride a Dragon's Storm
8. How to Break a Dragon's Heart
9. How to Steal a Dragon's Sword
10. How to Seize a Dragon's Jewel
11. How to Betray a Dragon's Hero
12. How to Fight a Dragon's Fury

JOIN HICCUP ON HIS QUEST
(although he doesn't quite realise he is on one yet...)

THE PROPHECY OF
THE KING'S LOST THINGS

'The Dragontime is coming
And only a King can save you now.
The King shall be the
Champion of Champions.

You shall know the King
By the King's Lost Things.
A fang-free dragon, my second-best sword,
My Roman shield,
An arrow-from-the-land-that-does-not-exist,
The heart's stone, the key-that-opens-all-locks,
The ticking-thing, the Throne, the Crown.

And last and best of all the ten,
The Dragon Jewel shall save all men.'

Hiccup

Camicazi

Snotface
Snotlout

Hiccup's best friend
FISHLEGS

↗ **TOOTHLESS**
Hiccup's disobedient little **dragon**

← Clueless and his hunting **FLAGON**

STOICK THE VAST
...cup's father and ... of the Hooligan Tribe (tough but dim)

MUM

I dedicate this book to my mother, Mavva

A big thank you to Andrea Malaskova and Judit Komar

HODDER CHILDREN'S BOOKS

First published in Great Britain in 2007 by Hodder & Stoughton
This edition published in 2017 by Hodder & Stoughton

5 7 9 10 8 6

SPECIAL EDITION

A CIP catalogue record for this book is available from the British Library.

ISBN: 978-1-444-93980-4

Cover design by Jennifer Stephenson
Background cover illustration by Christopher Gibbs

Printed and bound by Clays Ltd, St Ives Plc

The paper and board used in this book are made from wood from responsible sources.

MIX
From responsible sources
FSC
www.fsc.org   FSC® C104740

Hodder Children's Books
An imprint of Hachette Children's Group, Part of Hodder & Stoughton
Carmelite House, 50 Victoria Embankment, London EC4Y 0DZ
An Hachette UK Company
www.hachette.co.uk

The past is another land
And we cannot go to visit
So, if I say there were dragons
And men rode up upon their backs,
Who alive has been there
And can tell me I am wrong?

How to Twist a Dragon's Tale

written and illustrated by
CRESSIDA COWELL

Hodder
Children's
Books

A division of Hachette Children's Group

Map of the
during the ho
for 100 years

The Old Man in the Hole

The Omens are not good
The Volcano has awoken
The Exterminators are beginning to hatch
And they are flying through the dreams of one old Man
Who feels it is all his fault.
He has taken a vow of silence
And has placed himself in a deep hole
As penance
And so that he cannot interfere with Fate
As he did once, long ago.
He will come out when it is all over
If it is ever all over
      or
He will never speak again.

(The Volcano
has awoken)

Lava-Lout Island

Barbaric Archipelago,

test summer

. .

The Isle
of
Berk
is under
threat

How do you stop a
volcano from
EXPLODING??

~ CONTENTS ~

1. The Herding-Reindeer-on-Dragonback Lesson............17

2. The Exterminators..31

3. The Fire-Trap..53

4. The Fight...65

5. Who is the Man on the White Dragon?................72

6. Hiccup's Bardiguard Has a Busy Time...............97

7. The Tale of Humungously Hotshot the Bardiguard...121

8. The Twist in the Bardiguard's Tale................127

9. How Do You Take Advice from Someone Who Has
   Taken a Vow of Silence?..............................135

10. A Meeting of 'The Thing'.............................139

11. The-Quest-to-Stop-the-Volcano-From-Exploding.........157

12. Welcome to Lava-Lout Island........................162

13. Meanwhile, Back on Berk.............................172

14. Is it *Always* Nice to Bump into an Old
    Acquaintance?..175

15. Meanwhile, on *The Peregrine Falcon*...............193

16. I Didn't Mean to Come Here..........................198

17. Just Exactly *When* is Too Late?....................216

18. Can You Outrun an Exploding Volcano?...............220

19. Is the Universe a Good Egg or a Bad Egg?.........236

20. When the Play is Over.................................245

PROLOGUE

BY HICCUP HORRENDOUS HADDOCK III THE LAST OF THE GREAT VIKING HEROES

There were Heroes when I was a boy.

Now I am an old, old man, with white in my hair and wrinkles on my cheeks, it seems a long time ago.

So, I shall tell this story as if it happened to somebody else, because the boy I once was is so distant to me now, that he might as well be a stranger.

Here is the story of a Hero that I met when I was eleven years old, and about to embark on one of the most dangerous Quests of my Life, the Quest to Stop the Volcano from Exploding.

He was a very great man, but he didn't want to be a Hero anymore...

I am an EXTERMINATOR
Imprisoned in my Egg
I can see through
the clear transparent walls
of the shell I cannot break
After fifteen years
OF scratching
I look out upon the world
That I am dying to
IGNITE, and
Over the years, my fury
has been
simmering, stewing, boiling,
and now it is
SMOKING HOT

1. THE HERDING-REINDEER-ON-DRAGONBACK LESSON

Hiccup Horrendous Haddock the Third never forgot
the day he met an Exterminator Dragon for the very first
time.

How could he?

It was one of the most terrifying experiences of
his short, adventurous life.

There he was, sitting in the middle of a circle of
fire which was getting smaller and smaller, with no way
out, and prowling through the flames, getting closer
and closer, were these sinister leopard-like shapes, the
slinking silhouettes of Exterminator Dragons sharpening
their talons and getting ready to leap –

Hang on a second.

I had better start at the beginning.

It all took place during a heatwave in August,
which was surprising, for Augusts in the Viking
territories were normally rather cool, wet affairs. But
it had been growing hotter and hotter over the course
of the summer, and as the temperatures rose, Hiccup's
grandfather Old Wrinkly had been babbling on about
how the unexpected warmth was a terrible Omen of

Doom, and a new kind of Terror-Dragon had awoken in the West, and would descend upon them all with Fire and Destruction...

But unfortunately nobody really took Old Wrinkly seriously, because he wasn't very good at looking into the future.

On this particular day, the sun was beating down relentlessly on the usually soggy Isle of Berk as if it had lost its way, and thought it was in Africa.

There was not a cloud (let alone an Exterminator Dragon) in the sky.

Hiccup Horrendous Haddock the Third, only son of Chief Stoick the Vast, was on the Hooligan Pirate Training Programme on the Isle of Berk.

His teacher, Gobber the Belch, had decided that on this particularly still, stuffy summer's day, when all you *really* wanted to do was to find a nice tree and lie gasping underneath it, downing lots of drinking-horns of nice cool water, it would, in fact, be an EXCELLENT idea to hold a Herding-Reindeer-on-Dragonback lesson.

Hiccup did not agree with Gobber the Belch.

Clouds of midges →

But Gobber the Belch had not asked Hiccup's opinion on the matter.

And Gobber the Belch was a six-and-a-half-foot axe-wielding lunatic who was not the kind of teacher you argued with.

So there they all were, all twelve pupils on the Programme, standing in a hot, bedraggled, wilting line, halfway up Huge Hill, swatting off the midges that were gathering in great clouds in the still and steamy air.

There was Hiccup Horrendous Haddock the Third, rather surprisingly the Hero of this story, for he was extremely ordinary-looking, with bright-red hair that shot straight up in the air whatever you did to it, and no obvious Heroic qualities.

There was Hiccup's best friend Fishlegs, the only boy on the Pirate Training Programme who was even *worse* at being a Viking than Hiccup was. He had asthma, eczema, short-sight, flat-feet, knock-knees, an allergy to reptiles, heather, and animal fur, and he couldn't swim. He bore a strong resemblance to a runner-bean wearing glasses.

There was Snotface Snotlout. A delightful boy – if you happen to *like* unpleasant teenagers with skull tattoos who bully anything that moves and is smaller than them.

There was Tuffnut Junior. A pleasure to meet – if you happen to *like* meeting pimply young plug-uglies who pick their noses, and sleep with an axe under their pillows.

And Dogsbreath the Duhbrain, the largest, sweatiest, and smelliest of the lot of them, had all the grace and charm of a pig in a helmet.

There they all were, this horrid collection of spotty Viking pre-teens, and Gobber was shouting at them, in his usual cheery fashion.

Snotlout swatting the midges →

-ishlegs and Horrorcow ↓

22

'RIGHT!' yelled Gobber, the sweat pouring down his lobster-red cheeks and into his beard, turning it as limp and steamy as a jungle rainforest. 'I PRESUME YOU HAVE ALL BROUGHT YOUR HUNTING-DRAGONS?'

They had all brought their hunting-dragons. All except for Clueless,who really was so stupid that he shouldn't have been allowed out without a minder. He had brought his hunting FLAGON, which wasn't the same thing at all.

But everybody else had brought their hunting-dragons.

Most of the hunting-dragons were looking as cross at being called out on this mission as their Masters were, panting heavily with their forked tongues hanging out, and swishing their tails to keep off the midges and the flies.

Snotlout's dragon, Fireworm, who looked a bit like a flame-red Rottweiler with a face like a snooty alligator, was curling dangerously around Snotlout's legs, wondering whether she would get in trouble if she gave Gobber a big fat bite on his big fat hairy bottom.

If it was a big enough chomp, it might just stop the lesson while Gobber went to the Hospital Hut…

But, reluctantly, she decided that she *would* get in trouble.

Fishlegs's dragon, Horrorcow, the only vegetarian hunting-dragon anybody has ever heard of, had gone to sleep in Fishlegs's arms on the way up, and Fishlegs was trying to hold her head up in a way that looked like she was awake, and listening intently, because Gobber had strong views on how everybody at the lesson really ought to be conscious.

And all the other dragons were lounging at their Master's feet, or hovering limply a little way above their Master's heads, wishing they were somewhere else.

Hiccup's hunting-dragon, Toothless, was by far the smallest, a bright-green little Common-or-Garden dragon, about the size of a naughty dachshund, or Jack Russell terrier.

He was also the only dragon showing the same amount of enthusiasm for this expedition as Gobber.

He was fidgeting in and out of Hiccup's waistcoat in a whirl of impatience, scurrying up his shirt, his little claws tickling Hiccup's tummy, and then up out the collar and on to Hiccup's head. Then he would perch on Hiccup's helmet, spreading his wings and hooting in short, excitable bursts before scampering

24

back down Hiccup's body again.

'Are we s-s-starting yet? Are we s-s-starting?' chirped Toothless. *'When are we going to start? H-h-how many minutes? C-c-can T-T-Toothless go first? Me! Me! M-m-me!'*

'Calm down, Toothless,' said Hiccup, as Toothless accidentally stuck his claw up Hiccup's nostril on the way down. 'We've only just *got* here.' *

'OK, BOYS, LISTEN UP!' bellowed Gobber. 'Herding reindeer is a lot like herding sheep, but reindeer are bigger.'

Clueless put his hand up.

'*Which* is bigger?' asked Clueless.

'Sheep are the round fluffy ones, and reindeers are the larger ones with the pointy things on their heads,' explained Fishlegs kindly.

'Thank you, Fishlegs,' said Gobber. 'You will use your hunting-dragon to round up any stray reindeer that try to break away from the group we are herding. It's a chance to put into practise all that you have learnt in your Herding Sheep lessons.'

---

*Hiccup was the only Hooligan who could understand Dragonese, the language that dragons spoke to each other.

'I don't know how Hiccup the Useless is ever going to be the chief of this tribe,' sneered Snotlout, 'when he can't even keep control of that minuscule microbe of a dragon of his. Look what happened *last* Herding Sheep lesson.'

Toothless had lost his head on that occasion, and single-handedly CHARGED the flock, and chased it into the Dragon Toilets. (He claimed it was an accident, but Hiccup had his suspicions.)

It had taken three-quarters of an hour to get the sheep out of the Toilets, and they still stunk to high heaven four weeks later.

'But the main business of the herding,' continued Gobber, 'will be performed by YOU on your RIDING-DRAGONS...'

'C-c-can Toothless EAT the reindeer when he catches them?' squeaked Toothless.

'NOBODY is going to be EATING any reindeer, Toothless!' whispered Hiccup. 'And we're not going to chase them, either. This is *herding*, not chasing. We will just be *gently* guiding the reindeer in the right direction.'

'Oh,' said Toothless, hugely disappointed.

'... None of you have ridden dragons before,' Gobber boomed, 'and you will find it is more difficult

27

than you think. And therefore the dragons that you will be riding on today are NOT YET FULLY GROWN. This means that they will not have the strength to carry you up into the air.'

'Oh, *Sir*…' groaned Snotlout, 'I thought we were going to be FLYING today.'

'First you learn to ride,' said Gobber, 'and then later, MUCH LATER, you learn to fly. You fall off a flying dragon, Snotlout, and you will end up a SQUASHED Viking. Which would be difficult for me to explain to your father.'

'Can T-T-Toothless just eat a very small one?' asked Toothless, in a very small voice.

'No,' whispered Hiccup.

'So, ON our riding-dragons, we will approach the reindeer QUIETLY – no farting, Dogsbreath – and we will *carefully* surround the herd, and see whether we can guide it back towards Hooligan Village. Any questions so far? Yes, Clueless?'

'Which were the round fluffy ones again?' asked Clueless.

Gobber sighed.

'The round fluffy ones are the SHEEP, Clueless, they're the SHEEP. Now. You will find the riding-dragons rather a lively ride. They are just over here – *WHERE ARE THE RIDING-DRAGONS?* asked Gobber in exasperation. 'They were supposed to be following us.'

'I think they're over there, sir,' said Fishlegs, pointing to a small, twisted tree a little way away.

The riding-dragons were looking far from lively. They were lying in the shade, resting their heads on their paws, their forked tongues hanging out.

Gobber strode towards them, clapping his hands and shouting, 'COME ON, *UP* YOU GET THERE, YOU'RE SUPPOSED TO BE TERRIFYING, FOR THOR'S SAKE!'

And as the riding-dragons got to their feet, and slunk towards their Masters through the browned and shrivelled heather, like a pack of surly lions, Hiccup realised something that really WAS terrifying.

Something that gave a small indication that perhaps the day might take an unexpected turn.

The tree the riding-dragons had been sheltering under was blasted and twisted and reduced to carbon. All around the tree were scorch-marks. And when Hiccup moved a little closer to investigate, he found to his horror that the entire hillside behind had been burnt to a cinder and turned to sooty desert.

Where once heather grew and swayed in the wind, covered with butterflies and grasshoppers and buzzing nanodragons, now there was only ashy stubble, scarred across with white, stretching out across the whole of the slope.

Only one thing could do *that* to a hillside, and it wasn't the sun, however fiercely it might shine.

It was FIRE.

2. THE EXTERMINATORS

Hiccup swallowed hard.

'Oh dear, oh dear, oh dear, oh dear, oh DEAR,' he muttered to himself. '*What* has done *that*?'

Dragons, you see, were normally very careful about how they used their fire. They used it to fight and catch prey, but they would never dream of setting fire to a whole landscape. Why would they? It was the land that supported them, and gave them food, and shelter.

This must have been done by a 'Rogue Species', a different kind of dragon entirely.

Hiccup did not like to think of how dangerous such a dragon might be.

'Ummm, sir,' said Hiccup, 'I think you should come and have a look at this… I think there's been a dragon-fire here.'

'Dragon-fire? Nonsense and gull-droppings!' Gobber the Belch snorted, as he came to look at the destruction, his hands on his hips. 'This will have been caused by a spot of summer lightning.'

'There hasn't been a storm lately,' said Hiccup, 'and look,' Hiccup knelt in the dust, 'there's a sort of greenish tinge to the ash. It's definitely a Rogue Dragon Species.'

'*Thank you*, Hiccup,' said Gobber, with heavy sarcasm, 'for the helpful lecture, but I am the teacher here. GET BACK INTO LINE!'

Hiccup got back into line.

Snotlout smirked to see Hiccup being told off.

'No dragon, however Rogue, would DARE to attack us here in the Hooligan stronghold of Berk. The idea is RIDICULOUS, ABSURD, BIZARRE. It is not the done thing,' roared Gobber. 'Each of you mount your dragons! On the double, QUICK QUICK QUICK!'

Wartihog climbed on to his Marsh Tiger. Snotface Snotlout was riding the best dragon there, a smooth, evil-looking Devilish Dervish.

Tuffnut Junior had a Rocket Ripper with go-faster stripes along the sides.

'Hiccup the Useless and his fishlegged failure of a friend are really letting the rest of us down, Sir,' sneered Snotlout. 'Look at their pathetic riding-dragons. They're a disgrace to the tribe!'

Fishlegs and Hiccup had the runts of the group, one an ugly, cross little Chickenpoxer so fat its belly

The cross little Chickenpoxer

barely cleared the ground, the other a nervous
Windwalker with a wild look in its eye, and a
pronounced limp.

As the son of the Chief, Hiccup had first pick
when they went to choose their dragons from the
Dragon Stables a few days earlier. And he could have
chosen the Devilish Dervish Snotlout was smugly
sitting on right now, a superb, shining muscly creature,
who was clearly one day going to grow up into a
magnificent animal.

But something about the poor nervous Windwalker had caught Hiccup's eye.

He knew no one else would pick him.

And somehow he had the feeling that something awful had happened to the anxious creature lolloping crookedly in front of him. His legs bore the marks of having recently been in manacles.

'I wouldn't pick that one,' advised Nobber Nobrains, who was in charge of the Dragon Stables. 'We found HIM caught in a tree during a raid on Visithug Territory. We think he might be a runaway from the Lava-Lout Gold Mines, and runaways never make good riding-dragons. The kindest thing really might be just to bonk him on the head and have done with it...'

So Hiccup had picked the Windwalker with the limp.

Both Fishlegs and Hiccup did not quite believe that the fire had been caused by lightning, but there was no arguing with Gobber in this mood, so reluctantly they mounted their dragons.

Fishlegs's Chickenpoxer gave a furious snort, pawed the ground, and bucked Fishlegs off the moment he sat on his back.

'Yippee,' said Fishlegs morosely, as he got back on

board, and exactly the same thing happened again, only quicker, 'I can see I'm going to like dragon-riding...'

'*I* will be leading you on the back of my own dragon,' shouted Gobber.

Gobber's dragon was a great warty Bullrougher known as Goliath.

He winced as Gobber plumped heavily on to his back.

'Sweet chest hair of Thor...' grumbled Goliath. 'I do believe his bottom is even fatter than last week. It'll be a miracle if I can take off at all...'

'YOICKS!' yelled Gobber, squeezing his thighs to get Goliath going.

And the Herding-Reindeer-on-Dragonback party set off across the scorched wreckage of the heather, with Gobber enthusiastically shouting at the front, and everybody else following him in a more leisurely fashion.

Hiccup's Windwalker dragon didn't want to go after the others.

He was shivering all over and kept on looking up at the sky.

For some reason, the Windwalker seemed to have lost the power of speech, so Hiccup couldn't ask it what the matter was.

'It's all right, boy,' said Hiccup soothingly, his heart sinking. 'What's up with you? It's a lovely day, what are you frightened of?'

The Windwalker could not say, but he was certainly petrified of SOMETHING.

'C-C-COME ON!' bawled Toothless indignantly. Toothless lacked a sensitive side. 'Everybody else w-w-will have WON by now!'

'NOBODY is going to be winning, Toothless,' said Hiccup, patiently persuading the Windwalker to move on, and catch up with the others. 'Herding isn't a winning kind of thing.'

'OK. Toothless'll just scare the reindeer a little

... k-k-keep 'em on the run...' said Toothless.

An hour or so later, Gobber, flying on Goliath
and slightly ahead of the others, spotted the herd of
reindeer, nibbling quietly on the heather.

He immediately flew back to the straggling line
of boys on their dragons.

'Sssh, everyone, I've spotted the reindeer,' said
Gobber quietly. 'Now, we have to stay very relaxed
and orderly. We don't want to alarm them, and split up
the herd. Call your hunting-dragons to heel. Hiccup,
in particular, I want you to keep good control of
Toothless, we don't want a repeat of the Sheep-in-the-
Toilets incident.'

'No, sir. Toothless, did you hear that?' whispered
Hiccup sternly. 'You're going to stay very calm,
aren't you?'

Toothless shuffled along Hiccup's shoulders and looked deeply and solemnly into Hiccup's eyes. He nodded eagerly. 'Ohhhh, yes, yes, *yes*, T-T-Toothless will be v-v-very calm, oh yes.'

Hiccup blinked. Dragons' eyes are hypnotic, and he was already starting to feel dizzy. 'You promise?' whispered Hiccup.

'T-T-Toothless promises, cross his claws and hope to die...' And he licked Hiccup on the nose with his little forked tongue.

Hiccup took a good firm hold of the little dragon's body nonetheless.

To do Toothless justice, he did TRY to keep his promise, turning round on Hiccup's shoulder, so he wouldn't be tempted by seeing the herd, humming and attempting to think of things OTHER than reindeer – mice, for example, and fish, and interesting animals with cloven hooves... BOTHER... back to reindeer again.

All of the boys slowed
to a trot. Their hunting-dragons
hovered in the air, close behind them. 'These sheep have
got little pointy bits on their heads,' Clueless pointed out.

'That's because these sheep are REINDEER,
Clueless, Thor give me strength. Keep it steady there
… No sudden movements… Fishlegs, *try* and stay
the right way up… We just have to keep it *very*, *very*,
quiet…'

Toothless couldn't resist… he sneaked a peek
over his shoulder. There were the reindeer, so large, so
fat, so fascinating… standing there so dopily… What
would happen if he just stirred them up a bit…?

'*Toothless*…' whispered Hiccup warningly.

Toothless hurriedly faced the other way again.

'That's it, boys,' said Gobber delightedly. 'You're
doing a really good job now… they haven't startled at
all… we just have to keep riding calmly and silently for
a *few more minutes* and—'

'L-L-LET TOOTHLESS AT 'EM!' shrieked
Toothless, unable to bear it for *one moment* longer,
nipping Hiccup's fingers with his sharp little gums
to make him let go, and hurling himself at the herd,
screaming like a little banshee.

'Oh, for Thor's sake!' gasped Hiccup.

'*WHAT IN WODEN'S NAME IS YOUR DRAGON DOING, HICCUP, CAN'T YOU KEEP CONTROL OF HIM, CALL HIM BACK RIGHT NOW AND THAT IS AN* **ORDER***!!!!*' screeched Gobber in a furious strangled whisper. '*STOP HIM!!!*'

'Yes, sir, right away, sir,' groaned Hiccup, urging
the Windwalker forward after the charging little dragon
in the sky.

'TOOTHLESS!! STO-O-O-OP!!' cried Hiccup,

42.

trying to shout and be quiet at the same time, not easy.

Toothless gave a flick of his tail, and put his wings into 'blur' mode. This meant he could shoot forward, only slightly slower than the speed of sound. It also, usefully, cut out the noise of Hiccup screaming.

Toothless is just HERDING, explained Toothless to himself, as he sped through the air, *Just a little herding to keep those reindeer on their toes... they're loving it, look, they're smiling...*

He noticed, with delight, that the silly reindeer were beginning to run away.

'CH-CH-CH-CHARGE!!!!!!'

yelled Toothless, joyfully, as he flew.

'Thighslaps of Thor…' growled Gobber, pressing Goliath to speed up, 'the reindeer have started to run…'

C-C-CHARGE

And as Gobber raced faster, so too did the other boys, and within no time, all calmness had left the Herding-Reindeer-on-Dragonback party. They were a wild primeval sight, twelve boys on twelve dragons galloping across the heather, with Gobber the Belch screaming like a maniac flying above them at the front, and before him, the shrieking hunting-dragons, baying for blood like dogs.

'TO THE LEFT, HICCUP, KEEP TO THE LE-E-E-E-FT,' roared Gobber the Belch, as Hiccup disappeared into the distance on the back of his bolting Windwalker.

'Halt! Whoa! Left!' screeched Hiccup as the mad, tatty little scarecrow of a Windwalker, rocking crazily from side to side on his three legs, sped faster and faster.

Hooting furiously, Toothless hit the 360-strong herd of reindeer right bang slap wallop in the middle – which had the same effect as when the white ball firmly strikes the triangle of reds on a snooker table.

All 360 reindeers ricocheted off in 360 different directions, at 360 degrees of angles across the island.

cock-a-doodle-d-D-DOO!!

Toothless is so CLEVER!

'COCK-A-DOODLE-DOOOOOOO!!!!!!!!!!!' crowed Toothless in triumph. '*W-w-well herded, Toothless!*'

And then he did three victory somersaults in a row. '*S-s-stay and f-f-fight, you t-t-tree-headed COWS!*' he shouted insultingly after the disappearing reindeer bottoms.

Hiccup and the Windwalker came panting up, and halted with a screech.

'Too late!' sang Toothless. '*S-s-slowcoach! D-d-did you see? T-T-Toothless got them ALL, with one shot, Toothless is b-b-brilliant, Toothless is the winner, Toothless is—*'

'Toothless is VERY NAUGHTY,' finished Hiccup. '*I told you to stay calm, Toothless, I told you NOT to chase the reindeer, REMEMBER?*'

Ooooh, yes...
Toothless remembered now. He stuck his tail between his legs.

'*Toothless was h-h-herding...*' he said in a small voice.

Toothless is so SORRY.

47

'That was not HERDING, Toothless, that was CHASING!' scolded Hiccup.

Gobber was not pleased, to say the least.

'HICCUP has very kindly given us an exhibition of how NOT to herd reindeer. That is absolutely the OPPOSITE of what you should be doing. RIGHT. We'll just have to start ALL over again, won't we? From the beginning.'

'Oh Hic-cup,' groaned the boys, glowering furiously at Hiccup. 'Hiccup shows how USELESS he is, yet again,' snorted Snotlout triumphantly.

That was the start of an exhausting couple of hours.

Toothless got hot, and overtired, and hungry. As the afternoon wore on, the midges came out in great, biting clouds, and Toothless crawled under Hiccup's helmet to get away from them, from where he kept up a constant stream of echo-y complaints.

'Toothless go home now... is no f-f-fun any more...'

As the day wore on, however, the reindeer seemed to be re-forming into larger groups and the boys began to get the hang of working together with the hunting-dragons to guide the reindeers in the right

The little
chickenpoxer
bucking
Fishlegs
off for
the 15th
time...

direction. They were riding and herding much more expertly, and they were feeling extremely proud of themselves.

Fishlegs hadn't fallen off the Chickenpoxer for at least half an hour. And they had just managed to get control of a larger group of about sixteen or so reindeer, and were herding them down the mountain to the shore in a really rather professional manner.

Wartihog, Clueless and Tuffnut Junior were driving the herd from the back, calling and whooping and clapping to get the reindeer to move forward. And the other boys had split up and were riding on the right and left flanks, in semi-circles, so they were pushing the reindeer group along the path they wanted them to follow.

Snotlout whistled to Fireworm as a big stag made a break away from the group. And Fireworm swooped down, talons outstretched, trailing warning smoke, and the stag trotted away to fall back in with the rest of the crowd.

This was the life.

They were all wishing their fathers could see them now.

Hiccup rode along, nice and easy, with no hands,

feeling ten feet tall.

The reindeer poured down the mountain in a gleaming brown river, moving at a nice even pace. They cleared a small, dried-up stream, and bounded on downwards, into the woods, moving easily, evenly, very relaxed...

When SUDDENLY, the Leader of the Herd reared up in alarm as the woods in front of him burst into flames.

A long line of flames springing out of nowhere.

The reindeers bellowed in alarm and terror, and in a flurry of flaring nostrils, hooves and horns, they swerved past the fire and on down the mountain.

The Vikings were not so lucky.

By the time they reached the fire it was already burning three metres high.

'Quick!' yelled Gobber. 'Down to the shore! Run round the flames and down to the shore!'

But it was already too late.

In front of Hiccup's eyes the line of flame swooped across the entire landscape, moving faster than a man could run.

And then Hiccup saw the truly terrifying thing that he had been most afraid of, all along. Every single hair on his neck stood up like the spines on a sea-urchin.

There was something dark shooting through the trees, something that was making those flames.

Hiccup caught a brief glimpse of them.

Something like large black winged panthers, bounding low in the forest.

3. THE FIRE-TRAP

Only Gobber was riding a dragon big enough
to fly him over the fire and out of the
danger.

But there was no
question of him abandoning
his pupils, who were riding on
dragons whose wings were
TOO WEAK to take off.

They were trying desperately to do so, but only Snotlout's Devilish Dervish could muster up enough strength to carry him any height at all, before it collapsed to the ground again.

The Vikings on their dragons galloped down the line of flame, hoping to find a place weak enough to jump through.

But the woods were dry as a bone, and the fire burnt fierce and quick.

On and on the flames ran, and then they began to bend round in a circle, forcing the boys back and herding them up the hill, just as they had herded the reindeer only moments before.

The herders were becoming the herded.

Both ends of the circle of fire joined together.

They were now trapped on the top of the mountain.

All at the same time, the boys removed their swords from their scabbards.

Even the stupidest among them realised that they were now under attack.

The dragons were not terrified of the FIRE of course, for dragons' skins are fairly fire-proof,* and most dragons play in fire as joyfully as dolphins in water.

What the dragons did not like was those black shapes prowling IN the fire.

This is what terrified them, and sent them snarling backwards, their hackles rising. The boys dismounted their riding-dragons, for if they remained on their backs, there was a real danger the dragons would plunge them straight into the inferno in their fever to get away, for dragons are only obedient up to a certain point, and they will not stay and fight if their lives are in danger.

And, indeed, the instant the boys got off, the dragons fled upward, making Hiccup's heart sink even

---

*Sometimes completely, it depends on the dragon

lower, for dragons have a strong instinct for the presence of mortal danger.

One by one they fled, all of the riding-dragons – the Devilish Dervish, the Marsh Tiger, the Rocket Ripper, and with a final bad-mood, Shetland-ish snort, the Chickenpoxer.

All of the hunting-dragons – Fireworm (Snotlout's Monstrous Nightmare), Seaslug, Horrowcow, Forktail, Snakeheart, Bogflyer.

Until only Goliath was left.

And the Windwalker.

Rather surprisingly, for he had been running away all afternoon, now that there really *was* a reason to flee, the Windwalker stayed by Hiccup's side, its wings trembling and shaking nervously and looking over its shoulder.

Toothless, too, remained, hidden under Hiccup's helmet, and his muffled muttering could be heard echoing through the metal. 'D-d-don't know *why* we're here anyway... t-t-too midge-y... Toothless being bitten to death... Toothless thirsty... Toothless hungry... issa way past Toothless's bedtime, but n-n-nobody thinks of p-p-poor thirsty T-t-toothless, oh no, they're all so *s-s-selfish*, worrying about their own s-s-silly problems...'

The Vikings peered into the flames, up into the smoke-filled sky, waiting, waiting, waiting for the first strike.

It didn't take long.

There was a petrified scream from behind them.

They whipped around, just in time to see a reindeer fall down dead on the spot, from what looked like a long sword wound to the throat.

'What was that?' asked Fishlegs, quivering.

But no one could answer him, for it was too quick to see what had happened exactly.

'I think I saw something,' whispered Clueless, 'something black, a dragon maybe, came shooting out of the flames, killed the deer, and sprang back out of the circle again…'

Silence again, and the boys were rigid with tension, peering from left to right in the circle of smoke to try and guess where the next attack would come from.

Hiccup was sweating so hard he had to wipe his left palm on his waistcoat, because his sword was slipping in his hand.

And then there was another scream from

another reindeer, and again the boys whirled round, and again the reindeer was already dead, this time from sword wounds both to the heart and the head.

'OK,' said Gobber, 'we need to evacuate this area NOW.'

'How many of us can you take on your back at once, Goliath?' asked Hiccup.

'Two, I'd say,' grunted the big Bullrougher. 'One if it's a fatty like that one,' and he pointed a wing at Dogsbreath the Duhbrain.

'He said he could take two,' Hiccup told Gobber.

Interestingly, Gobber did not tell Hiccup off for speaking Dragonese in this emergency.

'Fishlegs and Speedifist,' ordered Gobber, 'get up on Goliath's back.'

The two boys scrambled up, and the big riding-dragon spread its wings and took off, up over the flame barrier, and out of the fire-trap.

Now the remaining Vikings had their work cut out trying to avoid being trampled to death by the hooves of the terrified reindeer, or speared by their antlers, as they panicked and stampeded around the circle, rearing up at the flames, and squealing in terror.

Silence again, and the boys were rigid with tension, peering from left to right of the circle of smoke.

Was it Hiccup's imagination, or did the circle of fire appear to be closing in on them?

By the time that Goliath returned, the flames were definitely inching forward, making the circle they were standing on ever so slightly smaller.

'Snotlout and Wartihog, you go next,' yelled Gobber the Belch.

Five times, Goliath flew out of the circle, with two boys on his back each time.

The sixth time he could only carry Dogsbreath the Duhbrain.

And the flames were burning higher than four tall trees on top of each other, terrible great towers, flaming all around them in a fiery circle so close that Hiccup's eyes watered and his cheeks burned as hot as if they were on fire already.

'Me tired,' complained Toothless from under Hiccup's helmet, still unaware of what was going on. 'W-w-when we going h-h-home?'

'I think *you* should go home *now*, Toothless, while you still can,' said Hiccup, trying to take his helmet off, but Toothless held it down with his gripping little claws and squealed in indignation. 'G-g-go away, m-m-mean Master, is too midge-y for poor Toothless out there, Toothless be eaten alive if he go out there!'

'Come on, Goliath, come on,' muttered Gobber the Belch, 'you great SLUG of a reptile, we're going to be Viking hamburgers at this rate, get a move on… ah, here he is, thank Thor.'

The great beast flew out of the flames up to the scrabbly pinnacle of mountain-top where the boy and his Master were kneeling. The boy's dragon, his Windwalker, was pressed up beside them both, with its wings outstretched, trying to protect them from the heat of the flames.

'On you go, boy,' growled Gobber the Belch, helping Hiccup on to the mighty dragon's back. He gave the boy a half-smile, and the Hooligan salute.

'See you across the other side,' said Gobber the Belch, as cheerfully as if he didn't know perfectly well that there probably wouldn't be time for Goliath to come back and rescue him as well.

That's a Viking Hero for you.

For perhaps, when Death was burning so close and so fierce only feet and minutes away from him, perhaps even Gobber was more frightened than he seemed to be.

But you couldn't
have told it from his face,
as he whistled carelessly
and slapped Goliath on the
backside for the last time. 'Off
you go, you Alligator-Featured
Slowcoach!' he roared.

'Out of my way then, Red-
Sprouting, Jelly-Bottomed, Walrus-
Face!' snorted Goliath in reply. The great
Bullrougher spread his wings and prepared
for take-off.

Nobody saw the black shape sneaking
out of the fire, leaping towards Goliath with a
flash of sword-like silver held out in front of it, and
springing back again.

It was as quick as that.

The powerful, roaring, barrel-chested dragon took

two strides forward… and sank to his knees, and on to his side.

He didn't make a sound, he just closed his eyes for the last time as gently as a baby, as soft as a sigh.

'Goliath!' cried Gobber in surprise, trying to lift up the great buffalo head in his bare arms. 'What are you doing, you idiotic animal? This is no time for sleeping!'

'He's not sleeping,' said Hiccup quietly, still sitting between the Bullrougher's tail spines. He pointed to the terrible green wound on Goliath's chest. 'I'm afraid he's dead, sir.'

Both boy and Master sat silently now, waiting for the fire to get them.

The great circle of flames burned high around their now-tiny patch of mountainside. A puff of wind could have blown the inferno across and snuffed them out in a heartbeat.

But perhaps it wouldn't be the fire that got them in the end, after all.

Now that victory was certain, now that the end was so close, the enemy hiding in the fire was prepared, finally, to show itself, to enjoy the final strike.

There was something moving in the fire.

Panther-like shapes crept through the flames, prowling round them, hunting them, watching them as a cat watches its prey.

4. THE FIGHT

Round and round the shapes circled, closer and closer, growling to each other in contentment, delighted with their victory.

Until finally one pushed its head through the flame.

It was a dragon, but not any dragon that Hiccup or Gobber had ever seen before. A dragon created by a god in a bad mood.

Fire licked from its blood-streaked eyeballs, came smoking off its forehead and crackling out of its nostrils. Its skin was semi-transparent, so that you could see the black veins bulging furiously in its temples, like a thick, pulsing spider's web.

It held its paws up in front of its face and...

ZING! ZING! ZING! ZING! ZING! ZING!

Six talons came shooting out of the ends of its stubby reptilian fingers, talons as long and broad and sharp as swords, and smoking hot.

Black saliva dropped slowly from its jaws. Green flames flickered up and down its talons. It bent down low in the fire, mouth agape, ready to spring at Hiccup, and...

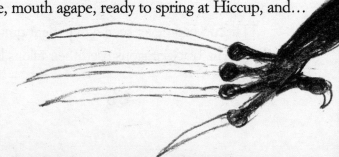

… and an expression of acute surprise came across its face.

And it disappeared back into the flames as quickly as it had emerged. For another, even more terrifying figure had sprung up in the inferno.

The figure of a pure-white dragon, with a single horn set in the middle of its forehead, rearing up, wings stretched wide. Astride its back was a gigantic Man with a sword on either hand.

But what MAN could ride into a bonfire and live?

Perhaps, Hiccup thought, *they had died and gone to Valhalla already, and this was Thor or Woden riding out to greet them.*

The black dragons had fallen back in shock, but now they re-formed, growling hideously, and in front of Hiccup and Gobber's disbelieving eyes, an astonishing fight began in the fire.

Hiccup had never seen a fight quite like it.

It was half dragon-fight, and half sword-fight, and the Man on the White Dragon was outnumbered six to one.

Hiccup had never seen a man fight quite like this Man. The black dragons used their talons like swords, springing at him from above, from aside, from below, slashing and thrusting.

The Man on the White Dragon had no shield, and he controlled his dragon with his knees alone. Roaring like a god, his arms moved so quickly that you could barely see them. His swords were there to meet every blow, every attack, every thrust.

'OK, Toothless come out now,' said Toothless, in a muffled way from beneath the helmet. 'Toothless need to do a p-p-pee-pee RIGHT NOW!'

'It's really not a good moment right now, Toothless,' said Hiccup nervously, holding his helmet firmly to his head. 'You should have gone earlier...'

'Let me out! Toothless c-c-come out now or Toothless do a pee-pee on Mean Master's H-H-HEAD!' screeched Toothless, furiously drumming his heels against the metal.

One second the Man on the White Dragon was parrying the lunges of twenty-four sword-talons simultaneously. The next his arms shot out to the left and right and two black dragons lay dead in the flames.

And all at once the remaining four abandoned the fight, shooting up into the air like gigantic dark bats, and the Man on the White Dragon galloped out of the

fire and into the circle where Hiccup, Gobber and the
Windwalker were crouching, and where Goliath lay dead.

'PERSON WITH THE ENORMOUS BELLY!'
roared the Man, taking off his cloak. 'Climb on the back
of my dragon!'

'The boy must go first,' said Gobber the Belch.

'Can't carry all of us!' bellowed the Man, above
the roaring of the greedy flames, creeping nearer and
nearer, 'but the boy will be safe, you have my word for it!'

'Swear,' said Gobber.

'I swear,' said the Man.

He threw Hiccup his cloak.

'Wrap yourself up in that, boy, and your own
dragon can carry you out of the fire.'

Slowly, Gobber stood up. Carefully, he removed his helmet from his head, and placed it very gently on the chest of the dead Goliath.

And only then did he climb on to the back of the White Dragon, which immediately leapt into the air.

'Wrap yourself tight!' the Man called down to Hiccup. 'It's fire-proof!'

Hiccup was alone in the circle of fire, so close now about him that his sleeve caught alight.

The flames surged forward to swallow up the last little piece of un-burnt land, as Hiccup leapt on to the Windwalker's back, pulling the cloak over his head, with both his sleeves burning.

The flames snuffed out instantly.

The cloak was as cold as the ocean and smelt comfortingly of fish.

It was like wrapping yourself up in the sea itself, and Hiccup gasped with the delighted shock of it.

He tucked the cool ends firmly around every part of him, so that not a finger, not a toe, not a morsel of his

body would be exposed to the fire. He threw his arms
around the Windwalker's shivering back.

'Run, Windwalker, run,' whispered Hiccup.
And as the whole of the mountain was consumed with
the flames, the Windwalker ran.

5. WHO IS THE MAN ON THE WHITE DRAGON?

Stoick the Vast was Hiccup's father, and the Chief of the Hairy Hooligan Tribe. He was a man built on generous lines, with a belly like a battleship, and a beard like an electrocuted Afghan hound.

He had been having a peaceful after-lunch nap in the surprising warmth of the afternoon, when he was rudely awoken by a couple of his Warriors chattering on about a fire up on the Highest Point... and how the Pirate Training Programme was up there herding reindeer.

Stoick immediately feared the worst. Stoick wasn't *normally* of a fearful nature, but his father-in-law, Old Wrinkly, who was a soothsayer, had been warning Stoick for WEEKS that the omens were saying that Hiccup was in danger.

Stoick had laughed this off, for Stoick was not a great thinker or worrier, even though for a small, skinny boy who didn't look up to much, Hiccup DID seem to get into an extraordinary number of dangerous situations.*

'CALL OUT THE FIRE BRIGADE!' bellowed

---

* See *How to Train Your Dragon*, *How to Be a Pirate*, *How to Speak Dragonese*, and *How to Cheat a Dragon's Curse*

Stoick, jumping out of bed and leaping for the door, dressed only in a rather fetching pair of hairy underpants that his wife Valhallarama had brought back for him from one of her Quests abroad.

When you live side by side with dragons you have to have an extremely efficient Fire Brigade System. Even though most dragons TRY not to fire-breathe unnecessarily, the hunting- and riding-dragons were always accidentally setting fire to the furniture or the thatch, and on these occasions the Fire Brigade could be on the scene in two minutes flat.

The Fire Brigade consisted of a whole fleet of Water Dragons, so called because their stomachs can distend to carry extraordinary amounts of water, ridden by Fire Warriors specifically trained in fighting fires. It took a little longer than two minutes on this occasion, for the Highest Point was some flying distance away from Hooligan Village, but within a relatively short space of time, the entire Brigade was there, the dragons swooping down into the seas below to scoop off huge amounts of water from the sea, and then shooting it out on to the blaze.

Their efforts were pretty hopeless of course, because this wasn't a tiny little matter of a hunting-

The Water Dragons

These extraordinary-looking creatures originate from the deserts of Asia. They store water in their humps (or in some cases, their stomachs) in much the same way as a camel.

~STATISTICS~

COLOURS: Sandy yellow, desert mustard
ARMED WITH: Powerful jets of water that can knock a person over
FEAR FACTOR:.......................2
ATTACK:...........................5
SPEED:.................................6
SIZE:....................................6
DISOBEDIENCE:....................2

dragon setting fire to a bedspread, but an entire burning mountainside, and by the time Stoick arrived, half naked on the back of his riding-dragon, the fire was flaming as strongly as ever.

Gloomily watching the blaze was a bedraggled line of pupils from the Pirate Training Programme, blackened and unrecognisable through the smoke.

'Hiccup?' stammered Stoick, dismounting from his riding-dragon, and wiping the smeariness from the face of the nearest boy in the pathetic hope that the soot-smothered young plug-ugly might be his son. *'WHERE IS HICCUP?'*

Sadly, Wartihog shook his head, and pointed a grubby arm at the mighty blaze in front of them.

'NO!' shouted Stoick, tearing his beard, staring at the blazing woods.

Out of the fire ran the Windwalker as fast as he could, and he came to a stop among the waiting Vikings. Hasty hands scrabbled at the cloak, unwrapping it with such speed that Hiccup fell out on to the heather.

He found himself looking straight up into the anxious face of his father, Stoick the Vast, and the heads of several other Warriors.

Behind those heads was the bright-blue sky, and

sliding down the flames

further
back
even than
that was
the flaming
Highest
Point, a great
funeral pyre for
Goliath and the
reindeer.

But not for
Hiccup – this time.

As Hiccup tumbled on to
his back, his helmet fell off,
and a hot, cross Toothless flew out.

'Mean, mean Master!' scolded Toothless.
'Hiccup VERY LUCKY nice, kind Toothless not do a
pee-pee on his head!'

But then the little dragon forgot his anger
immediately when he caught sight of the glorious
burning bonfire. 'OOOOOOhhhhh, FIRE!' squealed
Toothless in excitement, and he flapped off hurriedly to
play in the flames.

'He's alive!' bellowed Stoick the Vast in

astonished delight.

'*How* are you alive?' was Stoick's next, baffled question.

Hiccup pointed to something standing quietly some way beyond Stoick's shoulder.

The Man on the White Dragon, with Gobber sitting behind him.

'*He* saved me,' said Hiccup. Gobber clambered down from the White Dragon. He was totally black from eyebrows to toenails, apart from the small pink top of his bald helmet-less head, which shone in the sunlight like a halo.

hide-
and-seek
with
Horrorcow

'I can explain, Chief,' stammered Gobber.
'It was a perfectly harmless Herding-Reindeer-on-
Dragonback lesson, nothing dangerous about it at all,
and then we were attacked by these *things*... Goliath
didn't make it.'

'I am sorry, Gobber,' said Stoick the Vast
solemnly. Goliath had been Gobber's faithful riding-
dragon through many a terrible battle. 'We shall take
revenge on whatever did this, I assure you...'

'*He* saved us,' said Gobber, pointing at the Man.

'Who is *that*?' asked Stoick. 'Who is that Man?'

'He can't be a *man*,' pointed out Gobber. 'Men
don't walk through fire... He must be a god.'

'I'm not a god,' said the Man on the White
Dragon.

His voice was rather muffled by a black suit that
covered him from head to toe, even his eyes and mouth,
and Hiccup was wondering how he could see through it.

'I'm just a Hero – I mean an *ordinary bloke*, who
happened to be passing,' continued the Man. 'In fact
I'm in a bit of a hurry. I've got something important to
do now, so I must be off... Lovely to meet you and
everything... you seem like nice little people, in
your way.'

'You're a Lava-Lout!' roared Stoick, staring at the Man.

All the watching Hooligans gasped in horror, and drew their swords immediately. Lava-Louts were one of the Hooligan Tribe's deadliest enemies.

'I am not a Lava-Lout!' protested the Man indignantly. 'Lava-Louts are gorillas in trousers! And that's a bit of an insult to gorillas.'

'You are so a Lava-Lout!' exclaimed Stoick. 'Only low-down, double-crossing, mean-as-sharks Lava-Louts wear that kind of suit!'

The Hooligans growled in agreement, and pressed forward, waving their swords and checking the sharpness of their axe-edges, while crying out, 'Kill him! Kill him! Lava-Lout Vermin!'

'Bags I kill him first, Chief!' yelled Baggybum the Beerbelly. 'I haven't had a Lava-Lout in ages!'

'Get to the back of the queue, Baggybum you villain!' roared Tuffnut Senior. 'You're always pushing in front of everybody else!'

'I... AM... NOT... A... LAVA-LOUT!' howled the Man as loud as he could through his muffly headgear. 'Oh, for Thor's sake, you do a good deed, and see where it gets you! In the soup, yet again, why do I

never learn? *Bother* this Fire-Suit… I'll take it off and
then you'll see…'

The Man got down from his White Dragon,
and with both hands he pulled up the head section of the
suit he was wearing. It was stuck very tight, and made
rather a revolting squelchy, burpy noise as he peeled it
up.

'There you see!' said the Man triumphantly, as
with a final rude B-E-L-C-H he detached the headgear
from his face. 'NOT a Lava-Lout!'

Stoick walked slowly round and round the Man.
The head that he had revealed was clearly not the head
of a Lava-Lout.

It was the head of a blond, bearded, handsome
man, no, make that a *very* handsome man, slightly
past the prime of middle age, and currently looking
a little bit cross.

Stoick put his sword back in its scabbard.

'*Not* a Lava-Lout,' pronounced Stoick
with relief.

'But if not a Lava-Lout, then who are you?'

The Man looked extremely surprised.

'What do you mean… WHO AM I?' said the
Man. 'I'm HUMUNGOUSLY HOTSHOT, of course…'

Humungously Hotshot was one of the greatest Viking Heroes of recent times, who had completed such great Quests as 'the Slaying of the Rude Rippers' and 'the Fetching of the Weird Stone'. He had completely disappeared without trace fifteen years before, and everybody had rather assumed he was dead, which was an occupational hazard of being a great Viking Hero.

'No! Not Humungously Hotshot *the Hero*!' stammered Stoick the Vast in awe.

Suddenly, Stoick was rather aware of the fact that he was standing in front of one of the greatest Heroes of the Age, dressed only in a pair of hairy knickers and one rather ancient blue sock.

He sucked in his tummy, and tried to look his most dignified and Chiefly.

'But we all thought you were dead!'

'Yes, well,' said Humungous, frowning bitterly. 'I was on this Hero Quest in Lava-Lout territories and got caught red-handed by those Snakes-in-Helmets, the Lava-Louts. They slung me into one of their Jail-Forges, and so I've spent the last fifteen years underground forging swords for them. Which is why I'm wearing one of their Lava-Lout Fire-Suits. It's made out of dragon-skin, which means it's totally fire-proof.'

'They're *evilly* clever, those Lava-Louts,' said Stoick the Vast, shaking his head. 'How, by the great Hairy Thumbnails of Thor, did you ever escape?'

'Oh, I didn't escape,' explained Humungous. 'NOBODY escapes from the Lava-Louts. They evacuated the island. The Exterminators were hatching.'

'What ARE Extermi-whateveryousaid?' said Stoick. 'I've never heard of them before.'

'Exterminators are the Creatures who've made this little mess here,' explained Humungous, waving a hand at the scene of scorched devastation and fiery chaos behind him. 'They haven't been seen around these parts for centuries because their Eggs can only be hatched by the gases and lava given off by an exploding volcano. The Volcano on Lava-Lout Island has been grumbling away for a while now, getting ready for a really Massive Explosion, and when it does, all the Exterminator Eggs will hatch.'

'So you're saying they were EXTERMINATORS that attacked us just now?' asked Hiccup.

'That's right, I'd say about six small ones, baby Exterminators, you know, they were quite sweet really,' answered Humungous cheerily.

'And how many Exterminator Eggs are there left on Lava-Lout Island?' asked Hiccup.

82

LEARNING TO SPEAK DRAGONESE
BED TIME

Dragon: Toothless ava z-z-zuzzspook, Toothless uptime SNIP-SNAP.

Toothless had a nightmare, Toothless get up RIGHT NOW.

You (sleepily): May is di middling o di zuzztime!

But it's the middle of the night!

PAUSE

You (warningly): Na flicka-flame di sleepy-slab, Toothless, NA FLICKA-FLAME DI SLEEPY-SLAB! NA FLICKAFLAME – OH, Toothless!

Don't set fire to the bed, Toothless, DON'T SET FIRE TO THE BED! DON'T SET FIRE TO THE – OH, TOOTHLESS!

Dragon (delightedly): Hiccup izzup! Hiccup izzup! Hiccup tickla wit-Toothless?

Hiccup is up! Hiccup is up! Will you play with me?

no more than about nine hundred
d say,' nodded Humungous.

ll of this reminds me, I *am* in a bit of a hurry to
ge at of here. I'm so sorry to leave… you've all been so
kind… and if I were you, I'd leave too, and pretty quickly.
You don't want to be around when they hatch.'

'What are you *talking* about?' bellowed Stoick.
'LEAVE? There's no question of leaving. This is
our HOME. The Archipelago has been home to the
Barbarians ever since Great Hairybottom, the First
Barbarian of all, got off his ship and sank into the
bog right up to his thigh… He lost his boot on that
occasion… They never found it again… And that was
when he said those immortal words—'

'"There will be barbarians in the Archipelago for
as long as my boot is in that bog."' Hiccup finished up
the story, for he had heard it before. 'Yes, Father, I know,
Father, but AT THE TIME Great Hairybottom didn't
have NINE HUNDRED THOUSAND Exterminator
dragons about to fly down on the island and turn it
into desert.'

'That's not SO many,' roared Stoick the Vast.
'And they're only dragons, after all. We shall STAY,
and we shall FIGHT! I shall bring it up at the meeting

of 'The Thing'* which is in a week's time on Sun'sday Sunday, so that we can prepare to join together, and arm ourselves for the Battle to come.'

'Oh how I wish your darling mother was with us now,' sighed Stoick.

Hiccup's mother Valhallarama was a truly magnificent Warrior, but she was off Questing again.

'My little muscly sweetheart would CRUSH those Extermi-thingummys with one flick of her plaits,' said Stoick.

'WE WILL FIGHT THEM ON THE BEACHES!' he yelled. 'WE WILL FIGHT THEM IN THE BRACKEN! WE WILL FIGHT THEM IN THOSE BOGGY MARSHY BITS THAT ARE SO DIFFICULT TO WALK THROUGH WITHOUT LOSING YOUR SHOES! WE WILL NEVER SURRENDER!'

And then he broke into a rousing rendition of 'Rule Barbaria! Barbarians Rule the Waves', and every single Hooligan stood up straight and proud, and singing out the chorus at the top of their lungs while performing the Hooligan salute.

For a nation that spent a great deal of time

---

*'The Thing' was a meeting of all the local Tribes.

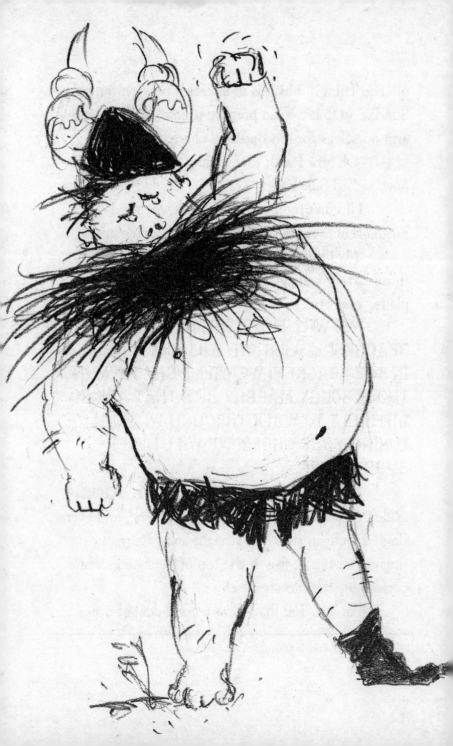

WE WILL
FIGHT THEM
ON THE BEACHES!
WE WILL FIGHT
THEM IN THE BRACKEN!
WE WILL FIGHT THEM
IN THOSE BOGGY
MARSHY BITS THAT
ARE SO DIFFICULT TO
WALK THROUGH WITHOUT
LOSING YOUR SHOES!
WE WILL
NEVER
SURRENDER!

fighting, burgling and ransacking, the Hooligans were a surprisingly musical lot. It was a shock to hear these ruffianly characters open their mouths, and the proud words come ringing out, pure and true, in perfect tune with each other, and in deep and gorgeous contrast to the scene of smoky devastation going on behind them.

Humungously Hotshot got up to go. He shook Stoick warmly by the hand. '*I* must say,' said Humungous, 'I think the clever thing to do would be to get out of here as fast as is humanly possible. But I have got to admire your suicidal bravery, mad and completely pointless as it is. Good luck, everybody!'

'Won't you stay and fight with us?' pressed Stoick the Vast. 'A great Hero like yourself would be a tremendous help.'

'Well, I think *now* I'm more of an Ex-Hero,' repeated Humungous. 'I'm just a Sword-for-Hire. No, I've had it with lost causes. It's all about ME, ME, ME from now on. But I do just have *one* last thing to do before I shoot off as far away from this doomed Archipelago as I can get. Could you possibly point me in the direction of the little Island of Berk?'

Stoick the Vast's face broke into a broad grin. 'But my dear Humungous!' he exclaimed, 'this IS the Isle of Berk!'

Humungously Hotshot's jaw dropped.

'*No!*' he said. 'Then you must be… you must be…'

'Chief Stoick the Vast!' cried Stoick the Vast.

'*Really?*' gasped Humungous, very politely NOT asking the question, *And do you* ALWAYS *prance around the mountainside dressed only in knickers and one blue sock?*

'And *this* is your son?' Humungous pointed at Hiccup.

'HICCUP HORRENDOUS HADDOCK THE THIRD!' roared Stoick the Vast proudly.

Humungous seemed to find this difficult to take in.

'THIS is *Hiccup Horrendous Haddock the Third?*'

Humungous turned to Stoick. 'You know, Stoick, I've changed my mind, I think I will hang around here for a while, after all.'

'Wonderful!' boomed Stoick. 'I think you said your new profession was a Sword-for-Hire?'

'That's right,' said Humungous.

'Well, I've been looking,' said Stoick thoughtfully, 'for a Bardiguard for my son, Hiccup.

HUMUNGOUSLY
HOTSHOT
as cool as a cat
twirling his whiskers

on a freshly frozen
iceberg.

You should be good at Bardiguarding, having once been a Hero.'

A Bardiguard was a bodyguard for the Heir to a Viking Chief.

Like a Hero, you were expected to be more than just a magnificent Warrior.

You had to be a complete all-rounder, good-looking, musical, handy on the harp, and just as good with the spear as you were with the axe. *And* you had to be a great teacher as well, because you were supposed to be instructing the young Heir in all these skills.

'How's your weapon-work?' asked Stoick.

For answer, Humungous drew his axe from his belt so quickly and so gracefully that Stoick didn't even see his hands move. He threw it sizzling through the air in such a way that it cut off one of Nobber Nobrains's plaits and then boomeranged back into Humungous's hand again, where he twiddled it twice around his wrist, balanced it for a moment on his elbow, and somersaulted it back into his belt again.

The Hooligans oooohed with pleasure.

There was nothing they enjoyed more than really

good weapon-work.

'WOW!' gasped Stoick.

This man was cooler than a cat twirling his whiskers on a freshly frozen iceberg.

'Oh, that was nothing,' said Humungous, sighing. 'In my younger days I could have done it *with my eyes shut.*'

'DON'T TRY IT,' growled Nobber Nobrains warningly.

'And I presume you're as good with everything else?' asked Stoick.

For answer, Humungous drew out his bow-and-arrow.

'You see that boy with the skull tattoos?'

Humungous pointed out Snotlout, who was standing some distance away chatting with Dogsbreath the Duhbrain, and picking his nose. Humungous let fly his arrow, and Snotlout fell backward with a short cry.

'My son!' exclaimed Baggybum the Beerbelly.

Humungous held up a humungous yet elegant hand.

'There is absolutely no cause for alarm, my dear sir. I think you will find that your son is completely unharmed. I have simply removed the

booger from his nostril.'

It was so. It had all happened so quickly, Snotlout just assumed he had been stung by a wasp, and went on talking to Dogsbreath, his nose bogey-free.

'But that's impossible!' stammered Stoick.

'*Child's play*,' said Humungous, shaking his head. 'The boy's nostrils are the largest I have ever seen.'

'And skiing? Dragon-riding? Bashyball skills?' asked Stoick.

'Nothing to what they were in my prime,' said Humungous sadly, 'but still tip-top, A-Grade, first-class. Us Ex-Heroes don't do mediocre.'

'Is it just *me*,' whispered Fishlegs, 'or is this guy really rather irritating?'

'It's just you,' said Hiccup, gazing at Humungous in total admiration.

'And harping?' asked Stoick. 'I am just assuming, with that magnificent waistline of yours, that you can sing a splendiferous Saga?'

'Once there was a lady,' sighed Humungous sadly, 'who claimed she would have DIED for my singing. Singing was my speciality, but NO MORE. Fifteen years working in those Jail-Forges, and my voice is completely broken. The gold-dust crept into my lungs, the heat

HEROIC SWORDFIGHTING TIPS

The Hypnotising switcheroo.

Make sure you do not confuse YOURSELF.

The old 'I do it better blindfolded feel-the-Force' trick

HEROIC SWORDFIGHTING TIPS

The Flash-kick
with-thrust
thingummy

Do be
careful of
your BACK.
Remember:
you are not as
young as you were.

95

burned out my voice-box. And worst of all, I have lost the will, the heart, the desire to do it… I will NEVER sing again.'

'That's a shame,' said Stoick, 'I do love a nice sing-song. Never mind. In every other way you seem perfect for the job. Will you be my son's Bardiguard? I will pay you handsomely.'

'I accept the post with pleasure,' said Humungous immediately. 'I'm saving up to buy a little farm somewhere quiet and out the way.'

'Excellent!' smiled Stoick the Vast. And Stoick bustled off, to call a meeting of the local Tribes, so he could form a War Party to fight the Exterminators.

'Will you teach me that Flash-thrust with twist thingy that you did in the Fire?' asked Hiccup, looking delightedly up at Humungous.

'Of course,' said his new Bardiguard, who was busy sharpening his sword.

6. HICCUP'S BARDIGUARD HAS A BUSY TIME

Stoick rather regretted hiring Humungous over the next couple of weeks.

Everybody, including Hiccup, seemed to think he was absolutely marvellous. He autographed axes, spears, favourite dragons, even Baggybum's famous beerbelly.

'Even his WRITING is humungously cool,' sighed Baggybum, gazing down at the stylish scrawl on his tummy. 'I'll never wash again…'

'Did you ever?' grunted Stoick, thinking, *Who does this Humungous guy think he IS?*

And that was the other thing.

Everybody normally followed Stoick's lead where it came to fashion.

That meant the beard was worn *au naturel*, in a tremendous tangly mess the size of a large and complicated bird's nest that had recently been attacked by a weasel.

The whole was then decorated with a lavish sprinkling of food droppings.

Suddenly, everybody was appearing with their

The Barbarian Fashion for BEARDS

Gobber's beard had turned into a riot of ringlets overnight...

Gobber's beard had turned into a riot of ringlets... overnight...

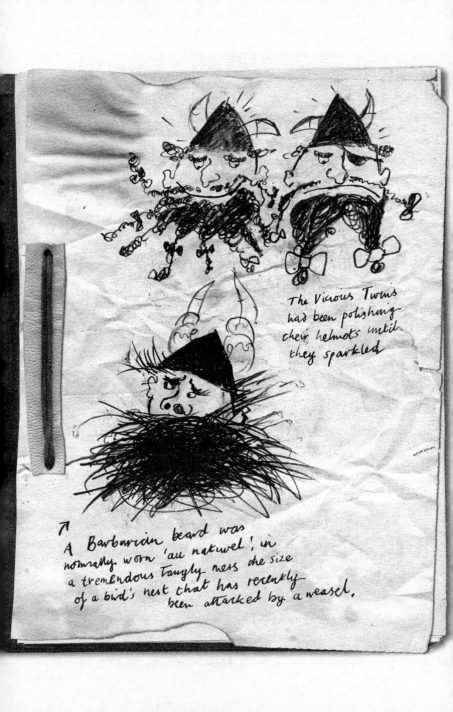

The Vicious Twins
had been polishing
their helmets until
they sparkled

↗ A Barbarian beard was
normally worn 'au naturel', in
a tremendous tangly mess the size
of a bird's nest that has recently
been attacked by a weasel.

beards immaculately groomed, just like Humungous's, and the ends of the moustaches elaborately twiddled and coaxed in pretty little curls. And Stoick strongly suspected they were WASHING, not to mention doing up their shirt buttons, and polishing their helmets till they shone.

'What have you done to your beard?' Stoick demanded of a rather guilty-looking Gobber, whose haystack had turned into a riot of ringlets overnight.

Gobber blushed.

'Oh *this*...' said Gobber carelessly. 'It's just the latest fashion, you know... more HEROIC... Everybody's doing it.'

'Well, you all look ridiculous,' blustered Stoick.

But what he found by far the most difficult part of the whole Bardiguard business, was that Hiccup seemed to look up to Humungous so much. It was all 'Humungous this' and 'Humungous that' nowadays.

Indeed, Hiccup *did* admire Humungous.

Here was a Hero a cut above the usual uncouth Barbarian. His fighting wasn't just the usual loutish bonking-on-the-head, but stylish, elegant, graceful.

He taught Hiccup the Flash-thrust-with-twist thingummy, and showed him how to tie an opponent into elaborate and beautiful knots, while at the same time courteously enquiring about the state of their health.

But Humungous was causing Hiccup the odd little difficulty, not his *fault*, of course, but there it was.

Hiccup's general practice on the Pirate Training Programme was to try and blend into the background and hope that nobody noticed him. But this is difficult if an exceptionally good-looking six-foot-seven internationally renowned Hero is following two steps behind you with his sword drawn and shouting out 'MAKE WAY FOR HICCUP HORRENDOUS HADDOCK THE THIRD, ONLY SON OF THE CHIEF!'

And there were other problems.

Gobber allowed the boys a bit of time off to recover from their Herding-Reindeer-on-Dragonback lesson, and then it was back to the normal Programme a day or so later, and an Axe-fighting-with-Art lesson.

The strange weather had, if anything, got even hotter. How hot could it get? It was like standing in the middle of an oven.

The boys stood in a straggly line in front of Gobber, scratching their bottoms, and sweating profusely. Above them towered Huge Hill, like a bad omen, its lower half alive with trees and ferns, its upper half a scalded desert, as bald and nude as Gobber's still-helmet-less-and-now-very-sunburnt head.

When Gobber the Belch asked for volunteers to fight Snotface Snotlout, there was a stony silence among the boys. Snotlout was horribly good at Axe-fighting, and he was a terrible cheat, who tended to kick you in the ankles with his specially sharpened sandals when Gobber wasn't looking.

So imagine Hiccup's horror when Humungous stepped forward, shouting out, 'I VOLUNTEER HICCUP HORRENDOUS HADDOCK THE THIRD, ONLY SON OF CHIEF STOICK THE VAST, O HEAR HIS NAME AND TREMBLE, UGH UGH!'

'SShhhhhh...' begged Hiccup. 'Please... pipe down...'

'Excellent idea!' bellowed Gobber happily. 'Hiccup is fighting Snotlout, then.'

'Oh, for Thor's sake,' groaned Hiccup miserably.

'What did you do *that* for?' hissed Fishlegs. 'You're his Bardiguard, you're supposed to be *looking after* him, not serving him up to his enemies on a plate...'

'What are you talking about?' said Humungous

in surprise. 'He's the son of a CHIEF, the hot fighting blood of the Horrendous Haddocks runs raging through his veins, he could take this guy Snotlout with one FLICK of his regal fingernails...'

'I don't know if you've noticed,' said Fishlegs, 'but Snotlout is nearly twice his size, he's as mean as a hornet with a grudge, and he HATES Hiccup.'

'Oh, I do,' grinned Snotlout, cracking his knuckles.

Snotlout happened to be the son of Baggybum the Beerbelly, who was Stoick the Vast's brother. This meant that if something were to happen to Hiccup, some tragic accident say, the next in line to the throne would be Snotface Snotlout.

Snotlout thought that he would make an EXCELLENT Chief of the Hairy Hooligan Tribe.

'Oh, come on, this Snotlout

Snotlout hates Hiccup

Snotlout!
Your axe
is
REAL!

guy is pitifully weedy!' snorted Humungous loudly. (This was unlike Humungous, for he was normally very polite.)

'T-T-Toothless bin saying that for years,' broke in Toothless excitedly, for he loved a good fight.

'Keep it down, please,' begged poor Hiccup, for Snotlout was hearing all this, and an even more spiteful look was coming into his eyes than normal.

'You'll smoosh this guy into the floor and have him *begging* for mercy, Hiccup!' cried Humungous.

'Let's just see WHO is going to be doing the begging…' snarled Snotlout from between gritted teeth, and rolling up his sleeves.

The boys practised their Axe-fighting with wooden axes in order to try and reduce the mortality rate. But somehow Humungous, who was helping Gobber by handing out the weapons, made matters even worse by handing Snotlout a real axe instead of the wooden one.

Both Snotlout and Hiccup realised this halfway through the fight when Snotlout's axe collided with Hiccup's shield and instead of bouncing off it, cut into the wood and stuck there.

A gleam of delight came into Snotlout's shark-like little eyes.

'*KILL* THE PIG-NOSTRILLED, JELLYFISH-HEARTED, WART-COVERED BULLY, HICCUP!' shouted Humungous helpfully from the sidelines.

'S-s-scratch his eyes out! Tear his wings off! Go for his h-h-horns!' squealed Toothless, flapping around getting in the way.

'Snotlout! Your axe is *real*!' shouted Hiccup.

'That's not my fault,' snarled Snotlout, 'everybody here saw your precious Bardiguard give it to me, so nobody's going to blame *me*...' and he yanked at the axe to get it out of Hiccup's shield.

Gobber was out of earshot, too busy yelling at Tuffnut Junior –

It was going to be a mistake to rely on Snotlout's sense of compassion

ANYBODY! HELP!

'THAT IS AN *AXE* FOR THOR'S SAKE, TUFFNUT, NOT A WOODEN SPOON, NOR A KNITTING NEEDLE...'

'HUMUNGOUS! HELP!' shouted Hiccup. 'You're doing a great job!' shouted Humungous, giving an encouraging and graceful thumbs-up. 'Keep up the good work! I think I saw tears in the Snotty-baby's eyes just then... Don't forget the Flash-thrust, it works just as well in axe-work.'

'*ANYONE!* HELP!!!!' cried Hiccup.

Fishlegs dropped his wooden axe and ran away from his fight with Clueless. 'HUMUNGOUS! Do something! That's a real axe Snotlout's got there!'

'There's no cause for alarm,' said Humungous calmly, as Snotlout dragged his axe out of Hiccup's shield, yanked the shield out of Hiccup's hands, and raised the shiny metal blade above his head. 'Hiccup has the situation completely under control. He's just lulling this thug into a false sense of security.'

'Are you a total MORON?' raged Fishlegs. 'Hiccup is about to DIE...'

Snotlout brought the wickedly sharp axe down towards Hiccup, Hiccup raised his own wooden axe up above his head to try and protect himself, and the metal axe just cut right through it, so that it split in two and fell to the floor.

The metal axe continued on down towards Hiccup's chest, Hiccup closed his eyes, waiting for the blow and...

... and in the nick of time, Humungous drew his own axe from his waistbelt with lightning swiftness, and he lopped Snotlout's axe off at the base so that the metal end fell harmlessly to the ground, while Toothless and Fishlegs dragged Snotlout backward by the seat of his trousers.

RRRRRIIIIP!!!!

Snotlout's trousers split from top to bottom, and Snotlout fled from the scene, half naked, followed by the loud laughter of his fellow students – I am afraid that Vikings have rather a basic sense of humour, and one of their number getting his trousers removed was just the kind of simple joke that really amused them.

'HA HA HA HA HA!'

chuckled the Hooligan boys, leaning on their axes.

'I'm sorry, Hiccup,' said Humungous, helping Hiccup up.

'Thank you,' gasped Hiccup, with a sigh of relief. 'What are you thanking *him* for?' squeaked Fishlegs in irritation. 'He's an IDIOT! An idiot with style, but still an idiot.'

'Shut up, Fishlegs, he saved my life for the SECOND TIME, didn't he?' said Hiccup.

Humungous looked uncomfortable.

The very next day, Hiccup was on the way to his Taking Money with Menaces lesson with Fishlegs. Humungous had wandered off a bit further up the mountain.

'I've packed,' Fishlegs was arguing. 'I think we should leave, you heard what Humungous said, that Volcano is going to blow any minute.'

'We can't just leave the rest of the Tribe here to get exterminated,' Hiccup replied anxiously. 'We have to persuade them somehow to come too...'

Fishlegs was just answering that there was NO WAY they were going to be able to persuade the Hooligans to do anything of the sort, because they were all too chronically stupid to understand the peril of the situation...

… when a large boulder mysteriously detached itself from the blackened hillside above.

It came crashing down towards Hiccup, and would have squashed him entirely, and that would have been the end of Hiccup, if Humungous hadn't called out from above at the last minute:

'LOOK OUT BELOW!!'

Hiccup and Fishlegs flung themselves to the left and the right, and the rock came crashing down in between the two of them.

'OhforThorssake… ohforThorssake … ohforThorssake…' gasped Fishlegs, sprawled on the ground and looking up at the dust clouds stirred up by the gigantic stone that had nearly killed them both.

'It's a sign, don't you see, it's a sign

from Woden that we really ought to be getting out of here… I'm going to go and check my packing again…'

'Sorry, guys!' said Humungous, hurrying down from the mountain above. 'My foot slipped and I must have knocked off a little bit of rock. Are you all right?'

'Well, we're still three-dimensional, and thank you for asking,' replied Fishlegs sarcastically. 'Oh, how I wish *I* had a nice smart Bardiguard all of my very own, to chuck rocks at me, and send me unarmed into one-to-one combat with teenage psychopaths.'

It seemed that perhaps Fishlegs might be right about the signs, however, because all these misfortunes, one after another, seemed rather foreboding.

Only the very next day after the rock incident, Hiccup was sitting down to a supper of oysters with his father. Humungous the Bardiguard was standing to attention behind Hiccup's chair. Toothless was underneath the very same chair quietly gobbling up an entire chicken that he'd nicked from the larder.

Stoick had finished his oysters before Hiccup had even *started* his, and was looking at his son's oysters, his mouth watering. His hands reached out for a particularly plump one…

… and Humungous shouted out, 'DON'T EAT

THAT OYSTER!'

Stoick looked at Humungous with Royal Disapproval. This guy was going TOO FAR this time. He'd got the whole Hooligan Tribe all decked out like girlies, and now he was trying to tell Stoick what to *eat*.

'I SHALL EAT WHATEVER OYSTER I LIKE!' roared Stoick the Vast, bringing the oyster up to his mouth. Humungous reached out, and made a grab for the oyster.

Stoick the Vast hung on in fury. There was an undignified scuffle, and Humungous had to swallow the oyster *himself* to prevent Stoick from eating it.

'RIGHT, THAT'S IT!' boomed Stoick the Vast, rather relieved, actually, to have hit on an excuse to sack the irritatingly perfect Humungous. 'YOU'RE FIRED!' Humungous finished swallowing. 'Bad oyster… very bad oyster…' he gulped. 'I could tell just by looking at it…'

'WOW!' gasped Hiccup. 'He just saved YOUR life, now, Father. He ate the bad oyster that *you* would have eaten! What a Hero!'

'Oh, yes, very good...' mumbled Stoick gruffly, thinking, *Just by looking at it, who is this maddening superman?*

'So he's not fired, is he, Father?' said Hiccup anxiously.

'No, I guess not,' said Stoick, thinking, *curses.*

'In fact, perhaps you should give him a MEDAL or something. Are you feeling all right, Humungous? You're looking awfully green.'

'I think perhaps, I should just have a little lie-down... for a moment, you know,' said Humungous, and he staggered out of the room, leaning on Hiccup's shoulder, with Hiccup chattering all the time, 'that was SO BRAVE, Humungous, and how could you tell it was bad, is it like mushrooms or something? I do hope you're going to be all right...'

Stoick pushed the oysters moodily away from him. He had quite lost his appetite.

Humungous was thoroughly ill for the next two days.

Which was just fine, as far as Stoick was concerned.

During this time, all the other Tribes began to arrive at the Meeting which the Vikings called 'The Thing', held to celebrate the mid-summer Festival known as Sun'sday Sunday.

The Bog-Burglars, the Meatheads, the Peaceables, the Grim-bods, the Bashem Oiks, the Silents and the Glums, the Terrormongers, and the Frothifists.

Everybody, in fact, apart from the Outcasts, the Rudeboys and the Lava-Louts, who were a totally lost cause.

Soon Hooligan Harbour was absolutely crammed with Viking ships, and the tiny island of Berk was jam-packed with tents of all colours of the rainbow. Market traders had set up shop in the sweltering, baking heat, trading ship-fulls of stuff, from octopus lollipops, to hunting bugles, to open-toed sandals, to dragon-skin bootees for your Viking baby who has everything.

The night before Sun'sday Sunday, Hiccup lay awake in the suffocating warmth for what seemed like ages and ages, as floating in through the window came the sounds of the Bashem-Oiks and the Bog-Burglars partying, and the shriek and scratch of dragon-fights.

Down at Hiccup's feet, Toothless lay awake too,

his claws stuck into his ears, wriggling and complaining, so wafting up in a muffled way from underneath the sheet came the sound of 'Isssssssssss r-r-ridiculous, R-R-IDICULOUS... b-b-barbarians... H-h-humans... s-s-so noisy... so s-s-selfish...'

But after a while the bedclothes fell silent, and the only sign of Toothless's presence was a warm little mound at Hiccup's feet that gently rose and fell, and the odd soft sleep-filled murmur of 'Isss r-r-ridiculous', accompanied by a little indignant smoke ring that crept out from under the sheet.

Hiccup watched the smoke rings as they rose up to the ceiling, or drifted slowly out the window into the sultry star-crammed night, and eventually he, too, fell asleep.

He dreamt uneasily, of fire, and omens, and dragons with talons like swords that pursued him through the hot feverish night.

In the middle of the night Hiccup woke up, with a silent scream.

There, standing beside the bed, stood the

terrible figure of Humungously Hotshot, standing over Hiccup like an Executioner, his two swords raised, poised to come down on Hiccup, his head in darkness.

He was muttering to himself loudly, in a voice that was awful to hear. 'Should I *do* it? Should I NOT? Should I do it? Should I NOT?'

'What are you doing?' asked Hiccup in terror. 'Bardiguard... STOP! What are you doing? Humungous! Humungous!'

Humungous appeared not to hear him. He went on talking to himself, in that awful voice, over and over again, something about a promise he had to keep.

He was wearing the hood of his Fire-Suit rolled down, so you couldn't see his face, or his eyes, which made it more awful still, and the moonlight glittered on the razor-sharp metal of his swords.

It was a dreadful moment.

Humungous's hands were shaking.

He brought them down.

He stopped them.

'I should NOT,' said Humungous, with decision.

Something shot out from the

118

sheet and bit Humungous heavily on the thigh with sharp, sleepy little gums.

Humungous let out a cry of pain and dropped one of his swords on his foot.

'ISSS R-R-RIDICULOUS!' snorted Toothless, sleep-flapping round the room for a bit. 'CAN'T A D-D-DRAGON GET ANY S-S-SLEEP AROUND HERE? YOU HUMANS SO N-N-NOISY! SO SELFISH! KEEPING POOR T-T-TOOTHLESS AWAKE ALL NIGHT...'

Toothless then crawled back under the covers and dropped off to sleep again.

Hiccup leapt out of bed, grabbing his sword from his scabbard as he did so.

Humungous hopped around the room holding his foot and his thigh.

'Ow ow ow ow ow ow ow...' cried Humungous.

The moment had passed.

All the fight had gone out of Humungous.

He peeled off the hood of his Fire-Suit, and now that Hiccup could see him in the moonlight, he didn't look scary any more.

He was still rather green from his illness and he looked very tired.

'I can't do it,' said Humungous. 'I gave my solemn, Hero's promise that I would kill you, but I can't do it. It doesn't feel right…'

'So you mean,' said Hiccup in astonishment, 'you're my Bardiguard, and you've been trying to *kill* me?'

'That's right,' said Humungous. 'I made a promise.'

Hiccup gave a slightly hysterical laugh.

Somehow it was very like Stoick to accidentally hire a Bardiguard who was supposed to be looking *after* his son, but was, in fact, trying to *kill* him.

'But WHO did you promise to kill me *for*?' whispered Hiccup. 'And why?'

Humungously Hotshot sighed. 'I see I will have to tell you my story,' he said.

And in the quiet stifling darkness of the night-time (for even the Bog-Burglars and the Bashem-Oiks had fallen asleep by now) Humungous the Bardiguard began to tell his tale.

7. THE TALE OF HUMUNGOUSLY HOTSHOT THE BARDIGUARD

'A long, long time ago, it seems like a lifetime away now,' said Humungously Hotshot, *'I was happy. I was a young Hero who fell in Love with a beautiful young woman.'*

'Uh-huh,' said Hiccup cautiously. He wasn't very interested in stories about Love.

'Oh, but she was beautiful!' sighed the Bardiguard. *'Her lovely fat, white, muscly legs! Her thunderous thighs! Her soft little beard! Her excellent sword-arm!'*

'Yes, yes,' said Hiccup hurriedly. 'Do get on with it.'

'She loved me back (or so I thought), but her father had some ridiculous idea that she should marry somebody CLEVER, I have no idea why THAT was important, so he set me an Impossible Task, which, if I completed, the reward would be her hand in marriage.

'The Impossible Task he set me,' said Humungously Hotshot, *'was to steal the Fire-Stone from Lava-Lout Island, and the reason that this is impossible is that the Lava-Louts have been looking for the Fire-Stone for many many years.*

121

'Before I set off on the Impossible Task, my Love and I met in secret. My little double-chinned Sweetheart had a singularly beautiful ruby, shaped like a heart, that she always wore around her neck. She had cut this ruby in half, and she gave one half to me, and kept the other.

' "Go on this Quest if you must," whispered my Darling. "But I have an awfully bad feeling about this, and if by any chance you happen to be captured by those pigs-in-pyjamas, the Lava-Louts, just send this ruby to me in the mouth of Xellence, your hunting-dragon, and I will come to rescue you."

'My Love, you see, was not half bad at Questing herself.

'I promised her, and rode off on my white dragon to carry out the Impossible Task, but by terrible bad Fortune I got caught by the Lava-Louts, just as my Love had feared, and my white dragon and I were thrown into chains, and into a jail on Lava-Lout Island.

'Even worse luck, my faithful hunting-dragon, Xellence, was killed during the Quest, and so I could not send the half-a-heart ruby to tell her I needed rescuing.

'For a couple of months I worked in

those Lava Jail Mines, utterly in despair. And then I made friends with this prison guard. His name was Terrific Al. He was such a nice guy, Hiccup. So smiley and sympathetic. I told him my story, and I asked him to take the heart-ruby to my lady-love and explain that I needed her to come and spring me from jail as quick as her dear, fat little legs could carry her.'

Humungously Hotshot's voice deepened and saddened. His face looked green and ill in the moonlight.

'Terrific Al said that he would do this for me, if I promised to do him a favour at some point in the future. He took the ruby heart and I waited in hope, Hiccup, in the heat of the mines, peering out of my barred window in the night-time, yearning for her to come. Days turned to Months. Months turned to Years. Hope turned to Despair. She never came. Fifteen years I waited, Hiccup. Fifteen years. And then, a couple of months ago, imagine my surprise when Terrific Al turned up on Lava-Lout Island as a prison guard again. One night he sought me out, and he told me what had happened to my ruby heart.'

Humungous's voice was so

take this ruby as a token, I promise you....

I will return, I promise you....

Humungous + Valhallavana
in L̲o̲v̲e̲

quiet now that Hiccup could hardly hear it.

'*Terrific Al told me that he had taken the ruby to my Love, and told her that I was captured, and needed rescuing. And to his surprise, my dearest Darling, who had sworn the solemnest oath of True Love For Ever, took that ruby heart and* THREW IT OUT OF THE WINDOW AND INTO THE SEA. *And as she did this, she said these heartless words:*

'"*There,' she said. "I already threw out the other half when I heard Humungously Hotshot had* FAILED *in his Impossible Task. I have found another Lover, who has already brought me the Fire-Stone, and I am going to marry* HIM.*"'*

'No!' cried Hiccup. 'How terrible of her!'

Humungous nodded sadly. 'Yes, I have never forgotten the words which Terrific Al repeated that day. They will remain with me as long as I live. And from that moment on, Hiccup, I vowed that I was through with Love.'

'I don't blame you!' said Hiccup.

And then a truly awful thought struck Hiccup, a thought that had Hiccup's heart sinking within his chest like half a ruby heart's stone sinking to the bottom of a sea-bed.

Suddenly he had a horrible feeling that he knew a way that this story might be going, a dreadful, snaking, corner coming up, a Twist in the Bardiguard's Tale.

'Um,' asked Hiccup nervously, really, *really* not sure that he wanted to know the answer to this question, 'what was the NAME of your lady-love, exactly?'

'My Ex-Lady-Love,' corrected Humungous. 'The name of my Treacherous Lady-Love was...

... Valhallarama.'

Valhallarama was Hiccup's mother.

8. THE TWIST IN THE BARDIGUARD'S TALE

'No,' whispered Hiccup. 'It's not true…'

'Yes,' replied Humungous, sighing, 'I'm afraid it is. And the story gets worse.'

'How can it get worse?' asked Hiccup through white lips.

'Your father did manage to steal the Stone. He found it INSIDE the Volcano, which was why the Lava-Louts had never discovered it before, despite digging holes all over the island. But what Al told me, was, that the Fire-Stone released certain chemicals that kept the Volcano dormant. Without these chemicals, over the last fifteen years, the Volcano has become more and more active, until finally, RIGHT NOW, it is ready to blow.'

Hiccup sat lost in thought.

While they were talking, the blackness at the window had turned to grey and then to turquoise, and the sun was coming up fast on what would be another roasting day.

'This Terrific Al of yours,' asked Hiccup, 'what is he doing *now*?'

'Well, he's gone a bit bananas, since you mention it,' admitted Humungous. 'But then the poor chap has had a difficult time of it.'

Humungous returned to his Tale.

'Shortly after Terrific Al returned as a prison guard, and as the rumbles from the Volcano were growing louder and louder, the Exterminators did start to hatch. The Lava-Louts abandoned the island, and left us prisoners to fend for ourselves, and we too made a bolt for it. All except for Terrific Al. He's got this wild idea in his head that he's going to TRAIN these creatures. He's built these gigantic statues all over the island, and he seems to think that when the Exterminators hatch they will think that he is their Leader, and will do everything he says.'

'And what is he going to do with the Exterminators once he's trained them?' asked Hiccup.

'Good Works, he says,' replied Humungous, shaking his head in admiration. 'He thinks he's going to stop them from killing everything in sight. Oh he's a lovely, lovely guy that Terrific Al, even if he is as mad as loon. Well, I tried to persuade him to leave with me but he wouldn't. And that was when he asked me to do the favour that I had promised him all those many years ago.'

The Exterminator

Exterminator Dragons are a Rogue Species of Dragon that are exceptionally dangerous. A pack of Exterminators lays waste an entire landscape by setting fire to it. They have large, sword-like talons, and two hearts. They kill for the pleasure of it.

~STATISTICS~

COLOURS: Skin that is slightly transparent so you can see their internal organs.
ARMED WITH: sword-talons, terrible fire.
FEAR FACTOR:...............9
ATTACK:...........................9
SPEED:........................9
SIZE:....................6
DISOBEDIENCE:......7

'What was the favour?' asked Hiccup.

'To kill YOU,' replied Humungously Hotshot. 'He said you were this PRINCE OF DARKNESS, a Devil Child, who would grow up to bring untold evil on the Archipelago. He said you had fed him to this Monstrous Strangulator that made all his hair fall out... And thrown him out of a balloon into a sea full of Ravenous Sharkworms...'

'That was all HIS fault!' protested Hiccup, who was beginning to put two and two together.

'But as I have got to know you, over the last couple of weeks, I have gradually begun to think that he must be mistaken in you,' said Humungous. 'I *tried* to kill you, but I kept on saving you at the last minute. At first I thought it must just be my Heroic Impulses kicking in, but then I realised – I *like* you, Hiccup.'

'Thank you,' said Hiccup.

'And I'm not angry with you about what happened. I'm not even angry with *her*... well, maybe just a little bit...' admitted Humungous, 'and why she had to marry that barbarian, Stoick, I will never know...'

'That's my father you're talking about!' warned Hiccup, 'and he has many excellent qualities, once you get to know him.'

'Well, I hate to let good old Al down,' said Humungous, 'but you seem to me like a Good Egg, and I think that Al has just got off on the wrong foot with you.'

'What does he LOOK like, this Terrific Al of yours?' asked Hiccup, already sure that he knew the answer.

'Fifteen years ago when I first met him he was extremely handsome,' replied Humungous. 'Tall, dark, took very good care of his moustache even in jail conditions. And he had all of his LIMBS at the time, which does help. Now… he's not so pretty. Bald, put a bit of weight on, a hook instead of a hand, a stump instead of a leg, a patch instead of an eye—'

'ALVIN THE TREACHEROUS, AS I LIVE AND BREATHE!' interrupted Hiccup. 'You gave your ruby heart's stone to ALVIN THE TREACHEROUS!!!'

Alvin the Treacherous was Hiccup's arch-enemy, and the wickedest, most dangerous man in the Archipelago. Hiccup had assumed he was dead when he fell into the sea with those Sharkworms, but Alvin was a difficult man to kill.

This meant that Valhallarama was not the traitor that Humungous thought her. Alvin would NEVER have delivered that ruby heart's stone. He would have pocketed it himself, and then made up all those wicked lies that he told Humungous about her throwing it into the ocean.

'Alvin the Who?' asked Humungous blankly. 'I don't know what you're talking about.'

'Alvin the Treacherous is the evilest man in the Archipelago,' said Hiccup.

'Now, then, that's not fair. Al has got you wrong, Hiccup, but you must admit, who can blame him, what with the Sharkworm incident and everything,' said Humungous. 'I just know if you guys could get together you would really get along.'

Hiccup sat thinking, wondering what he should do next.

'Now I understand why Old Wrinkly is sitting at the bottom of that hole,' said Hiccup.

'Who is Old Wrinkly?' asked Humungous.

'Old Wrinkly is Valhallarama's father,' said Hiccup, 'and my grandfather. He must have been the one who set you the Impossible Task of finding the Fire-Stone.'

'HA!' said Humungous bitterly. 'This whole mess is his fault in the first place!'

'Well, he obviously feels that too,' said Hiccup.

'About a month or so ago, he started talking about some DOOM coming on all of us, and how it was all his fault because he had interfered with Fate. And then he said he was going to take a Vow of Silence, and sit in a hole until the whole thing was over, for good or worse, so he couldn't interfere again.'

'None of us took a lot of notice at the time,' said Hiccup, 'because Old Wrinkly can be a little eccentric, but suddenly it's all crystal clear. I'm going to go and get his advice. Which will be tricky, because he has taken a Vow of Silence, but I have to try.' Hiccup woke up Toothless, put the sleepy little dragon on his shoulder, and turned to Humungous. 'Are you coming? You *are* still my Bardiguard.'

Humungous blushed. 'Are you sure you still *want* me to be your Bardiguard?'

'But of course,' said Hiccup. 'I think you are an excellent Bardiguard. Even when you were trying to kill me, you did a wonderful job of saving me from yourself. Will you shake hands?'

Humungously Hotshot's sad face lightened. He smiled.

They shook hands.

Time is ticking my way
The Volcano is shaking me daily

One day it shall shake me
Right out of my shell
and then I shall
BLAZE FORTH
with scorching red talons
and then . . .
Flames shall lap like water
Down the mountainsides
The trees will be crackling candles
stroking the sky with fiery fingers
And I shall turn all the flowers and small things
Into cinders and beautiful dust.

9. HOW DO YOU TAKE ADVICE FROM SOMEONE WHO HAS TAKEN A VOW OF SILENCE?

Old Wrinkly's hole was a dried-up old well about six foot wide and really quite deep. Hiccup had been visiting him every day anyway, bringing him food.

Hiccup carefully climbed down the ladder. It was quite a relief to get away from the clammy heat, and the further you went down, the cooler it became. His grandfather was already awake, and smoking his pipe on a small stool.

'I must say,' said Hiccup, as he sat down beside his grandfather, 'you have been very lucky in the weather. Most summers this hole would be ankle deep in water and mud at this time of year.' He cleared his throat awkwardly. 'I just found out about Humungous … and the Fire-Stone… and the Volcano… and everything that happened fifteen years ago.'

His grandfather turned his face away from Hiccup's.

'Now, *why* would Alvin the Treacherous want to have me killed?' wondered Hiccup aloud. 'He could just

sit tight on Lava-Lout Island, waiting for the Volcano to explode. He must think I'm going to do something to spoil his plans... but what CAN I do? I can't stop a volcano from exploding!'

Old Wrinkly stopped smoking for a second. picked up one of his books and rifled through the pages. He stopped on one page, and pointed with a bony finger.

THE RIDDLE OF LAVA-LOUT ISLAND, read Hiccup.

Through the open window came the clear sound of a bugle, calling all Vikings to a meeting of 'The Thing'. A meeting at which no one was allowed to speak unless they were holding the Fire-Stone... the very same Fire-Stone that Stoick the Vast had stolen from the Volcano, in order to win the hand of Valhallarama the Mightily Beautiful, fifteen long years before.

'THE FIRE-STONE!' shouted Hiccup. 'Maybe if we RETURN the Fire-Stone to the Volcano we can stop it from erupting!'

'Don't worry, Grandpa,' said Hiccup, 'I'll make it all all right.'

And Hiccup climbed the ladder back up to the real world.

The Riddle of Lava-Lout Island

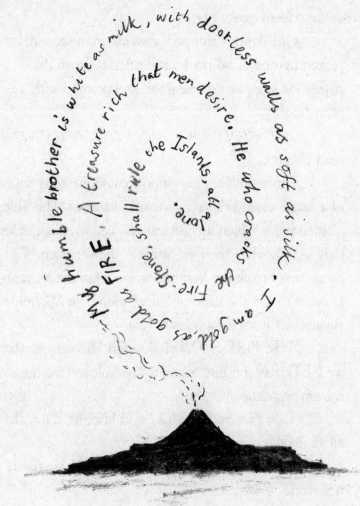

My humble brother is white as milk, with doorless walls as soft as silk. He who cracks the Fire-Stone, shall rule the Islands, all alone. I am gold as gold, as gold as FIRE. A treasure rich that men desire.

10. A MEETING OF 'THE THING'

'The Thing' was a real step forward for the Viking Tribes.

It took place in a gigantic circular dip on the slopes of Huge Hill. Steps had been cut into the dip, to make an enormous amphitheatre, and heather grew on the steps, which normally made them springy and comfy to sit on, but unfortunately due to circumstances beyond the organisers' control, this heather had recently been burnt to a cinder.

Everybody had to leave their weapons in a large heap before they entered the amphitheatre, just in case discussions got heated.

There was Madguts the Murderous, deep in discussion with Mogadon the Meathead, and his son Thuggory. Norbert the Nutjob, Chief of the Hysterics, fiddling nervously with his beard because he'd had to leave his axe outside so he didn't know what to do with his hands.

Grabbit the Grim was there, trying to hide from Big-Boobied Bertha because he'd rustled some of her reindeer a couple of months ago, and the sledgehammer fists and breathquenching breasts of Big-Boobied Bertha were the Terror of the Archipelago.

There was Deadlydog Dullard getting into a fist fight with Megalugs Mountain because Megalugs had laughed at his rather bright yellow leggings.

And there was Camicazi, Big-Boobied Bertha's tiny, tangle-haired daughter, gently pouring Itchyworms into the back of Grabbit's trousers without him even noticing, in secret retaliation for the reindeer-rustling incident mentioned earlier.

All around and above were the Vikings' dragons, snapping at each other, shrieking, tripping people up by running through their legs, and having to be pulled apart by their owners as they got into dragon-fights.

And right in the front row of this arguing, shouting, muscle-bound mess, sat Stoick the Vast, his chest puffed up with importance, swelling with pride and dignity.

Before him was a small plinth, and sitting on the plinth was the Fire-Stone.

And HE, Stoick the Vast, had stolen this Stone with his own fat hands, which made HIM the Big Man at this event.

'The Thing' couldn't take place without the Stone.

You had to be holding the Stone in

The Fire-Stone

order to speak, so that everybody didn't all talk at once.

The Hairy Scary Librarian blew the bugle. He took the golden Fire-Stone in his ancient old hands. 'WOULD THE PLAYERS PLEASE TAKE THEIR PLACES ON THE FIELD!' he wheezed.

The finest Warriors from every Tribe strode forward, flexing their muscles.

The amphitheatre exploded with noise as everybody sitting round about on the sooty seating yelled in support of their own Tribe. 'GO MEATHEADS GO!' 'KILL 'EM BASHEM-OIKS KILL 'EM!' 'VISI-THUGS, VISI-THUGS, VISI-THUGS!' etc. etc. etc.

The Hairy Scary Librarian blew the bugle again, and threw the Fire-Stone in the air.

All hell broke loose, with the Warriors on the field pushing and shoving each other out of the way to get underneath it, and the supporters on the benches shouting at the top of their lungs and barely able to control themselves from storming on to the pitch to join in.

Shortlegs of Glum had the slightly doubtful glory of catching the Stone.

And then both Shortlegs and the Fire-Stone

disappeared into a yelling scrum of muscly arms and legs and tattooed fists.

Stoick the Vast waited casually some way away, hovering near the plinth, confident that his Warriors would pull it out of the bag for him.

And, sure enough, after a few minutes, the hand of Gobber the Belch emerged from out of the heaving mass, chucking the Stone towards the larger of the Vicious Twins, who threw a long pass to Stoick the Vast…

… who dodged out of the way of Mogadon the Meathead, belly-charged Madguts the Murderous, caught the Stone in one fat hand, and touched it down on the plinth.

'TOUCH-DOOOOOOOWN!!!!!!!!!!!!!!' yelled the happy Hooligans. 'EVERYBODY QUIET! STO-*ICK*! ST*O-ICK!* STO-*ICK!*

Now the Rules of 'The Thing' said that everybody had to stay ABSOLUTELY STILL and silent while they listened to Stoick. The heaving mass of the Scrum had to stay absolutely as they were, legs and arms not-so-lovingly intertwined, while Stoick had his say.

Stoick the Vast, holding the Stone, cleared his throat importantly, and began to speak.

'Friends, Enemies, and Fellow-Barbarians!'

bellowed Stoick the Vast. 'We are all facing a Common Enemy today, an Enemy not seen in our Lands for hundreds and hundreds of years. These Extermi-whatsits are coming, and apparently there are a few of them. SHOULD WE *FLEE* LIKE THOSE COWARDLY BUNNY RABBITS THE LAVA-LOUTS?'

'NOOOOOOO!' bellowed the Vikings, drumming their feet on the incinerated heather. (You were allowed to reply, when asked a question.)

'Could you repeat that?' asked Shortlegs of Glum, from the very bottom of the scrum, for Grabbit's elbow was nestling in his ear-hole, and he couldn't hear a thing.

'I SAY WE *FIGHT!* screamed Stoick the Vast. 'ARE YOU WITH ME?'

'YAAAAAAAAY!' yelled everybody happily back at him.

'ARE WE THE KIND OF PEOPLE TO LET A PIDDLY LITTLE THING LIKE A TINY VOLCANIC ERUPTION GET US DOWN?' asked Stoick the Vast at full volume.

'NOOOOOOOOO!!!!' yelled back the Vikings.

'YOU BET YOUR BARNACLES WE

AREN'T!' yelled Stoick the Vast. 'FOR WE ARE
BARBARIANS, AND THE THING ABOUT
BARBARIANS IS, WE *NEVER* SURRENDER!
CAN YOU SING IT OUT FOR US BARBARIANS,
GUYS?'

All the Vikings jumped to their feet and sang
their hearts out, with Stoick conducting the chorus,
the Stone held like a Bashyball in one fat hand only:
'*RULE* BARBARIANS, BARBARIANS RULE THE
WAVES... VI-KINGS NEVER EVER EVER SHALL
BE SLAVES...'

Hiccup and Humungous had arrived at 'The
Thing' just after the second bugle had sounded, and
Humungous was watching the proceedings with his
mouth gently open.

Here was a version of democracy that he had
never even *dreamed* of.

'OK,' whispered Hiccup, 'my father's minute is
nearly up, I want you to go and hover near the plinth,
Humungous, and get ready to touch-down the Stone...'

'Righty-ho,' said Humungous, elegantly flexing his
humungous biceps. This looked like his sort of game.
Hiccup sidled up to Camicazi, who was cheering on the
Bog-Burglars.

Camicazi was a
friend of his, despite
the fact that she
belonged to
another Tribe.

'Camicazi,
can you do me a
favour, and nip
into the scrum
and pinch
the Stone for
me next time
they blow the bugle?'
Hiccup asked.

Camicazi getting
ready to do a little
BURGLARY

'But you're
on a different side!' exclaimed Camicazi in surprise.

'Oh, I'm not playing for the Hooligans,'
explained Hiccup. 'I've formed my own Team.'

'Oh, OK then,' said Camicazi excitedly. 'Thank
you for picking me!' She was a little fed up because her
mother Big-Boobied Bertha always said that she was too
small to play at 'The Thing'.

'I want you to nick that Stone, and then throw
it to that big good-looking bloke over there.' Hiccup

145

pointed at Humungous. 'Can you do it?'

'Of course I can *do it*,' snorted Camicazi, 'us Bog-Burglars can burgle ANYTHING. You should try stealing the underpants off Madguts the Murderous, this is easy-peasy in comparison. Watch and learn, Hiccup my boy, watch and learn…'

And Camicazi skipped off merrily towards the scrum.

The Hairy Scary Librarian blew the bugle, which was the signal that Stoick's one minute's talking was up.

There was a great roar from the crowd as Stoick threw the Stone up into the air. A forest of arms came leaping up out of the Scrum to catch it, and then the Stone disappeared again.

Stoick waited, confidently, for Gobber the Belch to bring the Stone out for him so that he could speak

again. Gobber the Belch was the best Bashyball player in the Archipelago, so Stoick and the Hooligans tended to dominate the proceedings at 'The Thing'.

However, to Stoick's immense surprise, when the golden Fire-Stone eventually emerged from the knot of bodies in the Scrum, it was in the arms of a tiny child with a great deal of long blonde hair, who wriggled out through the legs of a burly Visithug, neatly eluded the tackle of a great lumbering Bashem-Oik, and threw a truly magnificent long pass to…

… Humungously Hotshot, by the Armpits of Woden, what was *he* doing on the field, looking irritatingly Heroic and perfect as ever?

Stoick thundered towards Humungous, trying to

intercept the Stone.

I am afraid that Humungous couldn't resist the impulse to show off a little. He side-stepped Stoick, caught the Stone, juggled it from hand to hand while Stoick made clumsy grabs at it, twiddled it on the end of one finger tauntingly right in front of Stoick's nose, and then gracefully touched it down on the plinth.

Who can blame Humungous for that very gentle tease?

'TOUCH-DOOOOOOOWN!!!!!!!' roared the crowd. 'NICE STONE SKILLS!'

'NOT FAIR! WHOSE TEAM IS THIS GUY PLAYING FOR!?' bellowed Stoick the Vast.

Humungously Hotshot handed the Fire-Stone to Hiccup.

Hiccup cleared his throat awkwardly and stepped up to the plinth.

A Hero had to stay supple...

This was going to be hard.

'Um, he's playing for MY team. *Sorry*,
Father. LISTEN TO ME, FOR I AM HOLDING
THE STONE!' Hiccup called out. 'The plague of
Exterminators is going to be too strong for us to fight.
I'd like to introduce you to Humungous the Hero.'

There was a gasp of amazement from the

watching Viking Tribes, and cries of 'WOW! Humungous the Hero! Where has HE been for the last fifteen years?'

And 'Humungous the Hero – was he the one who went on the Quest to tame the Rude-Rippers? Ooh, look at his moustache, I wonder if I should wear mine like that...'

Hiccup held up his hand for silence. 'Humungous here has been on Lava-Lout Island, and he tells me there are THOUSANDS of these Exterminator Eggs, isn't that right, Humungous?'

Hiccup handed the Stone back to Humungous.

'That's right, guys,' agreed Humungous the Hero. 'HUNDREDS OF THOUSANDS... Trust me, there's no point in trying to fight these Creatures, Word of an Ex-Hero.'

That was enough for the Viking Tribes.

If Humungous the Hero, the bravest, coolest man in the Archipelago, who had slain the Rude-Rippers, who had fought the Slobberings, who had done a thousand daring Quests in his day, if HE thought they should flee, then it was clearly Fleeing-Time.

They leapt to their feet and thundered out of the Circle, Meatheads, Bashem-Oiks, Ugli-Thugs and all.

'HANG ON A SECOND!' yelled Hiccup. 'I'M

STILL HOLDING THE STONE! THIS ISN'T THE ONLY WAY, MY FATHER IS RIGHT ABOUT NOT SURRENDERING... WE COULD RETURN THE FIRE-STONE TO THE VOLCANO AND SEE WHETHER THAT STOPS IT FROM EXPLODING...'

But nobody was listening any more. Panic had set in, and now they were stampeding out of the Circle, down towards the Harbour, in a desperate hurry to get to their ships and out of the area.

'Errrr... what do we do now then, Chief?' asked Gobber the Belch.

Stoick was looking like a thundercloud.

'BETRAYED! BY MY OWN SON!' fumed Stoick the Vast.

Hiccup flinched.

Stoick removed the Stone from Hiccup's hands and drew himself up to his most impressive height.

'HICCUP HERE IS RUNNING AWAY,' shouted Stoick.

'No, Father,' said poor Hiccup, 'that ISN'T what I'm saying, please, will you just LISTEN, I think we should—'

'SILENCE!' roared Stoick. 'YOU HAVE HAD

YOUR SAY, HICCUP, AND NOW IT IS *I* WHO
AM HOLDING THE STONE!'

Hiccup was silent.

Stoick struggled to contain his anger, and then
continued speaking, with great Chiefly dignity. 'My son
is deserting, and you have my permission to follow him.
But *I* am going nowhere. I shall stay right here, and
fight to the bitter end. "Never Surrender" is the
Horrendous motto.'

The Hooligans looked at each other.

'And we shall fight with you!' yelled Snotlout.

And Hiccup looked on in total misery, as his
father patted a smirking Snotlout on the back, and told
him he was glad to see *someone* who had the spirit of the
Horrendous Haddocks in him.

'NEVER SURRENDER!' yelled the happy
Hooligans.

They all joined in a rousing musical chorus of
'These bogs are OUR bogs... these bogs are YOUR
bogs...', sung in male voices of such beauty, that
they would have set the gods a-weeping on their
thunderclouds.

'Oh brother,' moaned Hiccup, his shoulders
drooping.

'What are you doing still here, Hiccup?' asked his father sternly. 'I thought that you were leaving.'

Stoick pointed sternly towards the exit of the amphitheatre.

When they came out, Fishlegs was waiting for them, with his Running-Away Suitcase on his back.

'So?' he said eagerly. 'Everybody seems to be seeing sense at last, and getting out of here.'

'All except for us Hooligans,' said Hiccup gloomily. 'Apparently we Never Surrender.'

'Quite right, too,' said Camicazi, appearing out of nowhere, swinging her sword. 'I'm ashamed of us Bog-Burglars, running away like bunny rabbits at the first sign of a little danger. So, what's the plan, then, Hiccup? What does Team Hiccup do now, then, eh?'

'We can't leave without the other Hooligans,' said Hiccup. 'And they're clearly going to stay here whatever happens... in which case, we have to try and stop the Volcano exploding *ourselves*.'

Fishlegs's mouth dropped open. 'I don't believe I'm hearing this,' he said. 'Stop a Volcano exploding? How are we going to stop a Volcano exploding? With our bare hands? Ask it, pretty please?'

'If the Fire-Stone is powerful enough to keep a

volcano dormant for thousands and thousands of years,' said Hiccup, 'maybe if we RETURN it to the Volcano, then we can stop it from erupting...'

'Maybe!' squeaked Fishlegs. 'What happens if *not*?'

Hiccup said nothing.

'Oh *goodee!*' smiled Camicazi, absolutely delighted at the thought of a Truly Perilous Quest.

And from the front of her waistcoat she produced the Fire-Stone.

'Where did you get that?' gasped Hiccup.

'I nicked it from under Stoick's fat nose while he was busy singing,' said Camicazi breezily.

Humungous turned to go, but Hiccup stopped him.

'Where do you think *you're* going?' said Hiccup. 'I need you to show us the way to Lava-Lout Island.'

'I suppose I am still your Bardiguard,' said Humungous. 'But I will only go with you as far as the island. Climbing up the Volcano is Hero work, and I am out of the Hero Business for ever.'

'Right,' said Hiccup briskly, 'all we have to do now is borrow a fast boat, sail to Lava-Lout Island, chuck the Stone in the Volcano before it explodes, and sail back home again. Follow me.'

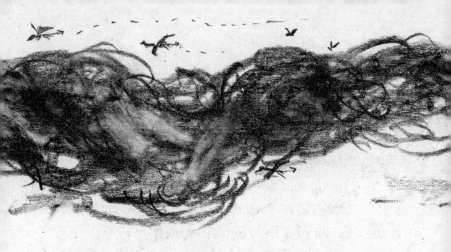

'That's *all* we have to do now?' squealed Fishlegs.

They had to fight their way through the crowds of fleeing Vikings at the Harbour.

The ship they borrowed, *The Peregrine Falcon*, was the fastest Hooligan ship in the fleet.

'We'll bring it back,' said Hiccup to himself, feeling very guilty, 'and if we don't... well, if we don't, it won't matter anyway.'

On that cheery note, with the sun climbing high in the sky on Sun'sday Sunday, Hiccup, Fishlegs, Camicazi, Humungously Hotshot the ex-Hero, Toothless, the Windwalker, and the White Dragon, sailed off out of Hooligan Harbour on the Quest-to-Stop-the-Volcano-from-Exploding.

11. THE-QUEST-TO-STOP-THE VOLCANO-FROM-EXPLODING

The Peregrine Falcon was a very fast ship.

It was still absolutely baking hot, but there was a feeling in the air that the weather was about to change, that it was building up for something stormy.

For months, the seas around Berk had been as eerily flat and glassy as a puddle. But overnight, a hot wind had sprung up, carrying with it large flakes of soot from the scorched devastation of the Highest Point and sending them flurrying across the Isle of Berk and out over the Sullen Sea like autumn leaves.

Only a couple of hours later, this sweltering wind had blown them right out of the Archipelago and into the Open Sea. There was a steady stream of dragons fleeing from Lava-Lout Island overhead, and they were joined by an ominous cloud of smoke coming from the same direction. Every now and then there was a rumble, but it was not clear whether it was thunder, or the Volcano.

I wish I could have explained to my father what I was doing... thought Hiccup, looking wistfully back at the outline of the Isle of Berk. Somehow, without meaning to, and while trying his hardest, he always seemed to be letting his father down. *I wish he didn't think I was a traitor... if we don't succeed, he'll think I really DID run away... If only he had LISTENED to what I was trying to say.*

Stoick rarely listened.

Fishlegs clung on to his Running-Away Suitcase, muttering to himself, 'This is not a good idea... this is not a good idea... this is not a good idea...'

'I'm not quite sure what the guy with the face like a fish is contributing to the Team, Hiccup,' whispered Humungous. 'You're the Leader, and the little blonde is the Stone-Carrier, but what is *he* doing? He seems rather a negative influence.'

'Don't be fooled by appearances,' Hiccup

whispered back. 'He *is* a Berserk.'

'Really?' said Humungous, in great surprise.
In his experience, Berserks were generally rather
LARGER, and did not normally suffer from asthma,
eczema, and knock-knees.

The Peregrine Falcon

Eventually the outline of Lava-Lout Island
appeared on the horizon, with its smoking Volcano, and
this was such an ominous sight that even Toothless lost
some of his cheekiness, and went to perch on Hiccup's
shoulder.

Misery seemed to have been trapped up in the

island for so long now, the land was trembling in feverish shivers; great reverberating trembles that rocked the sea crazily around it.

The roasted landscape was dotted with these greeny-yellow spots like pimples or pustules, as if they were symptoms of some deadly contagious disease, but as they drew nearer and nearer it became clear that these were not spots but Eggs, thousands and thousands of evil Exterminator Eggs, waiting for the Volcano to explode so they could hatch and spread their dusky devastation across the whole of the Archipelago.

They found a long scoop of a beach to land on, curved like a horse shoe, and *The Peregrine Falcon* skimmed across the shallow waters, until its belly landed on the black sand, and the boat came to a sludgy stop.

Clearly, the Windwalker was not going to set foot on the island.

Humungous sighed. 'I'll take the boat out a bit, and hang around, just in case… just in case…'

Humungous never finished the end of that sentence, but it lingered, unspoken, in the air… *just in case, by some outrageous miracle, you* DO *come back here alive.*

'Good luck, guys,' called Humungous.

The three small unlikely Heroes began to trudge reluctantly up the beach.

Fishlegs took his suitcase with him.

He knew that it was stupid, but somehow he felt a bit *safer* with his Running-Away Suitcase. It gave him courage. As if he could leave at a moment's notice if he wanted to. And, of course, he'd have some nice clean socks and knickers to change into when he got to Valhalla.

12. WELCOME TO LAVA-LOUT ISLAND

The Exterminator Eggs were so numerous that they found themselves picking their way through them. The Eggs had been laid hundreds of years earlier, so they were embedded very deeply into the soil, and grass, moss, heather and bracken had grown over them over the years. Now, however, all the vegetation had been burnt down, so it had exposed them like gigantic fat white maggots.

A furious, frenzied, scratching noise was coming from within them. It wasn't clear at first what this noise was, but as the Vikings climbed higher they began to come across Eggs that did not have the white, greasy opaqueness of bacon fat like their brother-Eggs further down.

These Eggs had skin that was wearing thin, and fine lines were appearing all over the surface, like cracks on china that was about to break. They were clearly close to hatching, and on some the shell was so fine that it had become see-through, and the Exterminator fledgeling was clearly visible within, all twisted and snarled in an angry knot.

162

These fledgelings had grown so large over the centuries, and were so cramped in their Egg prisons, that their limbs were contorted into the most grotesque positions, and it was the ends of their talons that were making that feverish scratching noise, as they tore at the hard shell exterior that was keeping them trapped.

Once you have looked into the eyes of an Exterminator, it is impossible to forget them. The look in an Exterminator's eyes, of pure, concentrated, white hot FURY, the irises vibrating with pinpoint anger, is a look that haunts a person through their waking hours and in their nightmares for ever after.

The Vikings had to climb over these horrible, slimy see-through Eggs, and as they did so the eyes of the Exterminators fixed upward on them in a frenzy of impotent rage, and the scratching became even more screechily furious.

'Oh... yuck... this is vile...' groaned Fishlegs, giving a shriek of horror as he slipped and fell with his face pressed up against one of the Eggs, with only that hard exterior separating him from the manic eye and madly scraping sword-talon of the Creature within.

Once he had made sure that the carnivores really *were* trapped inside the Eggs, Toothless couldn't resist

the opportunity of teasing them, of course.

He flapped right up and landed on the Eggs, sticking his tongue out and pulling faces at the imprisoned beasts, which drove them into extremities of temper, and they tried to throw themselves at him, but the most they could achieve, of course, was to make their Egg rock slightly in its bed of burnt-out carbon.

Toothless thought that this was a very good joke, and carried on doing it, despite Hiccup telling him repeatedly NOT to infuriate the Creatures any more than they had to.

Dragons have a cruel streak, and I'm afraid that Toothless even made up a song about the Exterminators, which he sang as he cheekily swooped over the Eggs making farting noises, and setting them rolling down the hill with his nose.

'Can't c-c-catch me
O w-w-weedy little Extermi-babies
Frogs without legs

164

Tadpoles in your cradles
I can see you crying in your Eggs
But you c-c-cant... catch... ME!'

Everywhere they walked there were these
grim entrances to the Fire-Gold Mines, out of which
great clouds of steam-mixed-with-gold-dust were
billowing. Hiccup swallowed hard, peering down
the sinister dark holes, cruel bright streams of
magma snaking through
the bottom of them,
and imagining
the poor
Windwalker
forced to crawl
down there,
struggling like a
fly without wings.

The Lava-
Lout Village gave
an even grimmer vision of what the life of Humungous
must have been like, kept for fifteen years as a slave by
these greedy savages.

There were CAGES everywhere, manacles,
chains, whips, weapons of all description. Huts with

barred windows, beds of stone or iron. No wonder poor Humungous didn't want to step on this cursed island again.

Hiccup, Fishlegs and Camicazi walked on, Fishlegs lagging slightly behind, puffing away like anything, but still stubbornly dragging his Running-Away Suitcase.

Every now and then they came across these unusual man-made Statues, of the kind that Humungously Hotshot had been describing, raised up high on a prominent rock so that they were clearly visible to all the Eggs round about.

They were Statues of a Face, three times as large as any man, and the Face did look just a *little* bit like what Hiccup remembered Alvin the Treacherous looking like.

But there was no sign of Alvin the Treacherous himself.

It had all been surprisingly easy so far.

They were now only four or five hundred metres from the top of the Volcano, and they had reached it without bumping into anything nasty at all.

All they had to do *now* was get to the summit, throw the Fire-Stone over the edge, and then run back down to the Harbour.

They were nearly there…

They were nearly there…

Only fifty metres to go, when Something put its black foot over the lip of the Volcano above them.

A black foot with five claws sprouting out of it, each claw as broad and sharp and gleaming as a SWORD.

Out of the top of the Volcano, like a gigantic slimy slug, slithered the revoltingly muscly figure of a huge EXTERMINATOR, three times as big as a lion. Green saliva frothed from its fangs. Great clouds of steam snorted out of its flaring furious nostrils.

Its face was contorted in a ghastly grimace of anger, eyes popping with a fury that burnt like acid. Its tail and its horns appeared to be on fire. It reared up on its hind legs, slicing through the air with its ten terrible sword-claws, and through the transparent wall of its fire-proof chest you could see its two great black hearts pumping its boiling-hot black blood, sending it shooting through its body at twenty times the speed and pressure of the blood of any other living creature.

It opened its terrible mouth to *ROAR*, and it was a noise that sent shivers screeching down the Vikings spines and set their hearts racing as quick as a panic-stricken rabbit's.

It seemed impossible that a Creature this wild could be controlled by a human being, but in the Exterminator's mouth was the choking copper-red slab of a metal bit, and on its back, in between its great ebony wings, rode the tall, sinister figure of a Man.

The Man had one arm that ended in a copper-red hook, and this hook was heaving on the metal reins as he fought to gain control of the enraged, rearing Creature. With the other arm he lashed at the Exterminator's sides with a great black whip until the dragon brought down its great front legs, and bowed down in snarling, pacing, barely controlled submission.

Fishlegs, Camicazi and Hiccup took a few steps backwards, Camicazi holding on very tightly to the Fire-Stone. The Man in Black pushed up the visor on his Fire-Suit.

The face below it was the same face they had seen on those gigantic statues littered over the island. A completely hairless face with no eyebrows, eyelashes or moustache. An unpleasant, glittering smile with too many teeth in it.

One eye piercing, as mean as a snake-bite. The other eye gone, and covered by an eye-patch.

One arm long, with a golden dragon bracelet writhing all around it.

The other arm short, ending in a hook like a copper-red question-mark.

'Good day, Hiccup Horrendous Haddock the Third,' drawled Alvin the Treacherous, quietly pushing his whip back into his waistband, unscrewing his hook and replacing it with his sword, the Stormblade. 'How absolutely *delightful* to bump into you again. And where might YOU three young scallywags be heading this lovely sunny Sunday afternoon?'

'Good day,

Hiccup H.H. III

13. MEANWHILE, BACK ON BERK

Meanwhile, back on Berk, at exactly the same moment that Alvin unscrewed his hook, a very gloomy Stoick had been standing with his Warriors around him, watching the crush of the deserting crowds at Hooligan Harbour.

His rather unpleasant nephew, Snotlout, came sidling up to him, an ingratiating smirk on his ugly mug.

'Humungous and Hiccup have already run away,' he sneered. 'And they've taken *The Peregrine Falcon*.'

'THE PEREGRINE FALCON?' roared Stoick the Vast. 'They've burgled my *Peregrine Falcon*?'

This was adding insult to injury.

Stoick the Vast loved his *Peregrine Falcon*. It was a beautiful blue and black narrowboat, the fastest in the Archipelago. Not only had that beastly thinks-he's-so-cool Humungous led his son astray with this cowardly Running-Away business, he'd had the cheek to do it in Stoick's favourite boat!

'Yup,' said Snotlout, gleefully fanning the flames of Stoick's wrath. 'I saw them only half an hour ago, sailing out of here to the west, as cool as you please.'

Stoick opened his mouth to explode.

And then he shut it again.

'To the west?' he said, baffled. 'Are you sure they were sailing to the *west*?'

He didn't wait for an answer. He swivelled round to the left, shielding his eyes from the sun with his hand.

There, disappearing over the western horizon, he could just see the curved white sail of *The Peregrine Falcon*. He would recognise that sail anywhere.

'Everybody else is deserting to the SOUTH!' bellowed Stoick. 'To the west is Lava-Lout Island, the Volcano and all those Extermi-whosits! What is my son doing deserting to the WEST?'

Stoick was not the brightest Barbarian in the business, but even *he* could see that this was a major mistake on the part of his son.

Gobber gave a little cough at Stoick's elbow. 'Um... I'm not sure he *is* deserting, Chief. Didn't you hear him say back there in 'The Thing' that he was going to take the Fire-Stone back to the Volcano to stop it from exploding?'

There was a short pause.

'Did he?' said Stoick eagerly.

Stoick didn't know what to think.

On the one hand he was over the moon that his
son wasn't deserting after all, and was NOT a traitor to
his Tribe, or a disgrace to the noble name of Haddock.

On the other hand, this was *insanity*.

Throwing the Fire-Stone back? Risking the
Volcano exploding, the Exterminators hatching...

It was ridiculous, mad, suicidal...

... why it was straight-down-the-line HOOLIGAN
HERO behaviour!

'WELL, WHAT ARE WE ALL DOING
HERE TWIDDLING OUR THUMBS FOR, THEN?'
roared Stoick. 'WE SHOULD BE *HELPING* THE
LAD! LAUNCH *THE BLUE WHALE!* GET
OUT MY BATTLE-AXE! (Thank you, Snotlout,
for bringing this to my attention.) DOWN TO THE
HARBOUR, ONE TWO ONE TWO ONE TWO!'

Curses, thought Snotlout. *Why did I open my
big mouth?*

14. IS IT *ALWAYS* NICE TO BUMP INTO AN OLD ACQUAINTANCE?

Hiccup would have been delighted to know that his father and the Hooligan Tribe were sailing to his assistance.

But they were still an hour or so's sail away, and in the meantime, Hiccup had more immediate problems.

Without even thinking, all three Vikings drew their swords as well.

Before doing this, Camicazi quietly removed her hairy waistcoat from around her shoulders, and carefully nestled the Fire-Stone inside it. (Alvin was performing the final twist on his sword, so he didn't notice her doing this, which is important, as we shall see.)

So near, and yet so far.

Fishlegs fumbled with his scabbard, in his haste to draw his sword, and the entire contents of his Running-Away Suitcase spilt all over the mountainside.

'Alvin the Treacherous!' blurted out Camicazi. 'How on earth did you escape from all those Sharkworms?'*

---

*To find out about Alvin and the Sharkworms, please read *How to Speak Dragonese*. Another excellent book.

'So kind of you to ask, my dear young lady,' murmured Alvin the Treacherous, picking at his teeth with the end of his hook, for all the world as if he was relaxing in an easy chair, rather than sitting on the back of an Exterminator, on top of a Volcano that was about to explode. 'So kind of you to ask. After you had torn down my precious Fort Sinister and thrown me to the Sharkworms, most people would assume that I would *indeed* be dead.'

Alvin's one eye was now cold and furious.

'We didn't *throw* you to the Sharkworms!' protested Fishlegs. 'You *fell*, in the middle of trying to kill us!'

Alvin ignored him. 'But you should know that a Treacherous is hard to kill, my dears, very hard to kill. The Sharkworms were hungry but I was hungrier. The first Sharkworm took my eye,' Alvin pointed savagely at his eye-patch, 'but it regretted it,' said Alvin with grim satisfaction. 'I killed it as it ate, from a single blow of the Stormblade, and then I crawled inside its open mouth, and hid within the floating corpse while the feeding frenzy continued.'

'Oh, yuck,' groaned Fishlegs, pulling a face.

'Indeed,' bit Alvin, 'but one finds one is not so

picky when one's life is on the line. Six long hours the frenzy continued, before the Sharkworms started to drift away, along the Summer Current. And then, my hook curled around the floating Sharkworm's backbone, I struck out for the shore. It took me a long time, for we had drifted far,' said Alvin bitterly, 'and weak and eyeless as I was. And then when I *finally* managed to get within swimming distance of the land, and let go of the dead Creature that had hidden me, and supported me that whole way, it took one final act of revenge. Even though it was long since dead, its jaws snapped forward in a reflex action, and took off one of my kicking, swimming legs from just below the knee.'

'Oh, dear,' murmured Hiccup, sympathetic, even though it was Alvin.

'Quite so,' said Alvin. 'All of the Romans had left by the time I got back to the Island. So I spent that long cold winter hiding in the ruins of Fort Sinister, nursing myself back to health, practising my sword-fighting, and dreaming of REVENGE.'

'Oh *dear*,' said Hiccup again.

'Quite so,' said Alvin again. 'I have my revenge on the SHARKWORM. I have carved my fake leg out of the tooth with which it bit me. But I do not have my revenge on YOU, Hiccup Horrendous Haddock the Third. You owe me a hand, a leg, an eye, and a full head of hair, and I intend you to pay.'

'But it is not strictly my fault that you lost all these things!' protested Hiccup. 'You brought them on yourself! And speaking of owing people things, what about YOUR treatment of poor Humungously Hotshot? You took his ruby heart's stone, and left him to rot in the terrible Gold Mines of this island. You let him think that his Love did not love him, and had married someone else knowing that he was still alive, and in slavery. What had Humungous done to *you* for you to hate him so badly?'

'I can hate without reason,' spat Alvin the Treacherous. 'And what about his treatment of ME? He promised me that he would kill you. That would have been such a lovely artistic twist of Fate, to kill his Love's only son, I would have enjoyed that so much.

'And I worked so hard for it, pouring poisonous

178

lies about you into his foolish trusting ears, stoking up his ANGER and his bitterness, his desire for revenge... I never expected a Hero like him would break a solemn promise like that one, especially to ME, whom he owed so much. My goodness,' Alvin sounded virtuously indignant, 'you can't trust anybody these days!'

Alvin sighed. 'But I suppose if he failed me in killing YOU, Hiccup, he has also failed me in the second part of his mission.'

'What was the second part of his mission?' asked Hiccup in surprise.

Alvin's hairless eyebrows lifted. 'Didn't he tell you?' purred Alvin. 'I wonder why not? He was supposed to bring the FIRE-STONE to me, here, at the Volcano.'

Camicazi, Hiccup and Fishlegs all gasped and took a step backward, horribly aware that the Fire-Stone was lying only a few feet behind them, curled up in Camicazi's waistcoat.

'The Fire-Stone?' stammered Hiccup, playing for time. 'What's the Fire-Stone?'

'You know perfectly well what the Fire-Stone is, Hiccup,' sneered Alvin. 'The Fire-Stone has many powerful secrets, but one of its many riddles is that the Exterminators are terrified of it. So he who holds the Fire-Stone controls the Exterminators... and therefore the Archipelago. I wonder why Humungous didn't tell you he was supposed to bring it to me.'

Alvin looked with narrowed eye at the three young Vikings, all trying to look unconcerned.

And then Alvin smiled, as something occurred to him, a silky serpentine smile, revealing far too many teeth. 'Perhaps it is because *you were bringing it to me anyway*!'

Alvin started to laugh, throwing his head back in a singularly unpleasant gloating roar. 'Oh this is TOO GOOD!'

He wiped his streaming eyes.

'You're a clever boy, aren't you, Hiccup? Perhaps you worked out another of the Fire-Stone's riddles... that it can stop the Volcano from exploding. So you have come here, three terrifying Viking Heroes, none of you taller than my armpit, bringing the Fire-Stone with you, hoping, praying, *longing* to prevent disaster at the last minute! How swe-e-e-et...' Alvin sneered.

He moved a little closer to the three Vikings, like

tut tut. I do so HATE to
disappoint the little children
in their charming little dreams...

a malevolent spider, swishing his Stormblade and tut-tutting insincerely.

'And you were so close,' he commiserated, 's-o-o-o-o-oo close to success! So near… and yet so far. What a *shame*. I do so hate to disappoint the little children in their charming little dreams.' He sighed. 'But I'm afraid it can't be helped. It's my job.' A hint of steel crept into his voice. *'Hand over the Fire-Stone, Hiccup.'*

'I haven't *got* the Fire-Stone,' said Hiccup stoutly.

'Really?' asked Alvin in disbelief.

Toothless had crept out from under Hiccup's helmet and was listening with interest. 'Oh y-y-yes you have!' he stammered. 'It's right over—'

Hiccup hurriedly clapped a hand over his mouth. Alvin chuckled, for he understood enough Dragonese to know what Toothless had just said.

'You're a clever boy, Hiccup,' he said, 'but you really should have learnt by now to work alone, like me. Then you wouldn't be let down by all the idiotically stupid creatures and people around you… HAND OVER THE FIRE-STONE BEFORE I LOSE MY TEMPER!'

'NEVER!' yelled Hiccup.

Alvin the Treacherous leapt at Hiccup. 'YOU

CATCH THE OTHER TWO, EXTERMINATOR,
ALIVE, MIND YOU, I NEED THAT FIRE-STONE,
AND LEAVE HICCUP TO ME!'

The Exterminator swooped forward towards
Camicazi and Fishlegs with a savage growl, and reared
up on its hind legs, its ten sword-claws spread out in
front of it.

Hiccup held up his sword, Endeavour, in the
very nick of time, and it caught the Stormblade as Alvin
brought it down towards Hiccup's chest with terrifying
ferocity.

Camicazi and Fishlegs were fighting a Great
Black Monster with ten swords to their two. The
Creature used its claws just exactly as if it were sword-
fighting, and its fingers were so flexible and bendy that
they moved like arms, thrusting delicately in and out.

It wasn't under orders to kill them, thank Thor,
only capture them, and within about two minutes it had
done just that to Fishlegs, with its left arm.

One finger sent Fishlegs's sword spinning up
into the air to disarm him. With its left leg it knocked
Fishlegs down, and then it pinned Fishlegs to the
ground with its five sword-fingers, two above his
shoulders, and two below his arms.

It had more trouble with Camicazi, for Camicazi was a wonderful sword-fighter, and she chatted the entire time she fought, which was even more off-putting than the sword-fighting itself.

'Take *that*, you Slow-coach, Serpent-Tongued, See-Through-Chested Hand-bag!' she cried, leaping through its swords, and tweaking its whiskers. The Exterminator howled in pain and fury.

'Cry-baby!' cried Camicazi joyfully. 'Does the ickle Dwagon-Monster want his ickle Mumsie to kiss it better for him den?'

A look come into the Exterminator's eyes, which said as plain as day, 'Maybe I should kill this little gnat after all, WHATEVER my Leader says.'

The Exterminator swelled up in fury, and redoubled the slashing and thrusting of his five razor-sharp blades, and eventually he broke through her guard, picked her up, kicking and screaming, and pinned her down with his five sword-fingers plunged into the ground around her, just like he had done with Fishlegs.

The Exterminator wasn't so bothered by her insults now she was at its mercy, and it lay down its gigantic, oozing,

Fishlegs's Running-Away Suitcase →

pantherish body in between Fishlegs and Camicazi, and folded up its great black wings to watch the fight between Hiccup and Alvin.

'Humungous was right,' said Fishlegs to Camicazi gloomily. 'There *is* no point in having me in the Team. I did TRY to make myself go Berserk, but it only works when I don't want it to. At least *you* put up a fight, and you burgled the Stone and everything. *I've* done nothing helpful at all. I might just as well have run away like the others.'

This wasn't quite true.

Sometimes we can be helpful in ways that are not totally obvious, and if Fishlegs had run away like the others, he would have taken his Running-Away Suitcase with him, and that Suitcase, as we shall see, was about to come in extremely useful.

Alvin had been practising his sword-fighting since the last time Hiccup fought him, on top of the mounds of Treasure in the Caliban Caves.

But then Hiccup had been practising too, and had been getting extra sword-fighting lessons with Gormless the Grim, because it was the only thing on the Pirate Training Programme that he was at all good at.

a very rare Example of a Viking umbrella

And although Alvin was taller and had longer arms than Hiccup, he did have the disadvantage of the ivory Sharkworm-tooth leg, which made him stagger about the mountain-top, cursing horribly, while Hiccup was very light on his feet, and quick to dodge even the most violent of thrusts.

It was very evenly matched.

But Alvin had one other advantage over Hiccup, which was that he was a big CHEAT.

It is not considered good

sportsmanship, in Barbarian Culture, to make a huge swipe at your child-opponent with your hook while sword-fighting.

Nor is it thought to be part of the Viking Code to trip the pre-teen up with your Sharkworm-tooth leg as he dodges out of the way.

However Alvin had never been a good sport, and he did both those things, in quick succession, without so much as a twinge of guilt.

Hiccup sprawled on to his backside, arms and legs flailing.

With a howl of triumph, Alvin the Treacherous hauled the sword, Endeavour, out of Hiccup's hand, and threw it far out of reach.

As Alvin wrenched the sword from Hiccup's hand, and raised the Stormblade for the final blow, a flash of sunlight caught the bracelet writhing around Alvin's good arm. This would have been the end of Hiccup's Quest, had he not had the good fortune to have landed right in the middle of the spilled contents of Fishlegs's Running-Away Suitcase.

Still sprawled on his back, Hiccup grabbed hold of the nearest thing to him, which happened to be a box of Fishlegs's tooth powder, and flung the entire contents of the box up into Alvin's face.

'Yoooooooooooowwwwwwwww!!!!!!!!!!!!' screeched Alvin. Fishlegs's tooth powder was one of Old Wrinkly's most popular medicines, a mixture of extract of seaweed, gull droppings, and spearmint for the taste. I don't know what actual good it did for the *teeth*, but it certainly stung like crazy as it worked its way into Alvin's one good eye.

While Alvin stood there, momentarily blinded,

Hiccup jumped up and pulled the bracelet off Alvin's arm. It took a few mighty tugs, for it was stuck fast to the Fire-Suit, but Hiccup was desperate, and pulled with a strength he didn't know he had. He threw the bracelet up to Toothless, shouting, 'Take that to Humungous!'

Toothless caught the bracelet, heavy as it was, and sank like a stone, nearly to the ground. Mouth full of bracelet, he began to stammer out 'W-w-why???'

'JUST DO IT!!!! DON'T ARGUE FOR ONCE IN YOUR LIFE!' howled Hiccup. '*FAST!!!*'

the weight of the golden bracelet making him sink even faster

So the little dragon pointed himself down towards the tiny speck of *The Peregrine Falcon* floating in the bay, and shot towards it, the weight of the golden bracelet helping him sink through the air even faster.

Meanwhile, Alvin could now just about see out of his streaming red eye and he was after Hiccup again, as mad as a snake with toothache.

Hiccup held up the suitcase as a shield as Alvin rained down blow after blow, finally cutting the thing practically in two. Hiccup just rolled out of the way in time.

Alvin grabbed hold of his waistcoat, and Hiccup wriggled out of it, hitting Alvin on the nose with a sightseeing book called *Visiting Rome for the First Time*.

'*You* should have learnt a lesson from your silly old grandfather. *He's* learnt not to try and interfere with Fate. And he thought he was clever enough to hold the Fire-Stone!' snarled Alvin.

'All HIS meddling, his silly Quests, achieved were to break his daughter's heart... I wish you could have seen how Valhallarama cried when I told her that Humungous was dead... Oh, it was tragic.'

'Liar! Traitor! Villain!' shouted Hiccup, dodging

Place in nostrils and inhale

yet another of Alvin's lunges and looking about
him for something else that could be used as a
weapon.

'Oh, BOO-HOO,' sneered Alvin the
Treacherous, creeping forward, his eye glittering,
'stop, you're going to make me CRY.'

Old
Wrinkly
Asthma
Pot 1016

And then Hiccup threw one thing at him
after another, the entire contents of Fishlegs's
Running-Away Suitcase, that were now lying all
around them on the mountainside.

Fishlegs's belt, whose heavy gold buckle
caught Alvin full in the forehead, six pairs of
clean knickers, several pairs of trousers, a bottle
of asthma medicine, which made both of them
sneeze, and Fishlegs's pillow, which burst on the
end of the Stormblade, and showered the two
of them in a rain of goose feathers.

'Ow, ow ow!' screeched Alvin, as
Fishlegs's hairbrush landed bristle-side up on
Alvin's sensitive chin, and one of Fishlegs's vests
got caught around his ivory leg.

But although Hiccup put off his defeat

One of Fishlegs's vests
caught around Alvin's leg →

for vital minutes, particularly with a spirited fight using Fishlegs's umbrella instead of a sword, the end was never really in doubt.

Alvin was determined that Hiccup was not going to slip out of his fingers this time. Stumbling and staggering, his eye watering, and spitting out goose feathers, he chopped the umbrella in half and finally got Hiccup in a hold he couldn't wriggle out of.

'Now!' gloated Alvin, bringing the Stormblade down to Hiccup's face. 'Where is the Fire-Stone?'

Now, where is the Fire-Stone?

15. MEANWHILE, ON *THE PEREGRINE FALCON*

Meanwhile, Humungous had spent an anxious half-hour down on *The Peregrine Falcon*, shading his hands over his eyes and trying to spot the progress of the three young Vikings as they slowly climbed the Volcano Mountain.

What he discovered was that it was FAR more tense watching somebody else performing a Quest than it is to do the Quest oneself. He felt quite sick with nerves.

Most of the time he was talking to himself as he peered upward, trying to convince himself he was doing the right thing.

'Now, I was *right* not to tell Hiccup that Terrific Al wanted that Stone too, wasn't I? And nobody could expect me to go with them, could they?... After fifteen years of slavery on this very island... but I guess nobody else is going to do it, but for Thor's sake,' Humungous slung his bow-and-arrows around his shoulders, 'a guy should get to retire SOMETIME, shouldn't he? UP now, White Dragon... I mean, why is it always ME who has to be the Hero?

'It's... not... my... fight...' complained

Humungous, taking his foot out of the stirrup again.

He turned his face to the heavens and howled up to the uncaring sky, shaking his fist in frustration:

'WHAT... SHALL... I... DO?????'

And as if in answer to his question, out of the clear blue sky, DOWN swooped an exhausted little Toothless, and dropped upon the deck a golden something.

A something that rolled around the deck in ever-decreasing circles, and came to rest with a clatter.

Humungous bent down and picked up the something.

It was the golden dragon bracelet that twisted around Alvin's good arm. He knew it well, for he had made it for Alvin himself, in the Jail-Forges when he was supposed to be making swords, as a thank you after Alvin agreed to take the ruby heart's stone to Valhallarama many many years ago. This was the first time in a long while that he had seen it close up.

And as he picked it up, he thought, *That's funny, there's something in the dragon's eye. I didn't put that there when I made it...*

And as he held it closer, a blast of lightning lit up the sky, and the flash of light caught the bracelet, and the dragon's eye winked at him.

One small, sly, red wink, as if it were amused.

The dragon's eye was his ruby heart's stone.

In that single moment the Truth rushed upon
Humungous all at once.

She *had* loved him.

She had never got the message.

Terrific Al had never given it to her.

He had kept the ruby heart's stone… he had even had the cheek to fit it into the bracelet that Humungous had made him, which he had then been wearing right under Humungous's nose the *entire time*… which made him a whole lot less Terrific than Humungous had thought.

Maybe it even made him the Treacherous Villain that Hiccup had been describing… and perhaps throwing him to the Sharkworms was a THOROUGHLY good idea and what a shame they had only taken his leg and hadn't got rid of him completely.

A fifteen-year-old memory popped into his head.

It was a memory of his Love, handing him this very stone so very many years ago.

With these words:

'*When you hold this stone, you hold my heart. But if you find yourself captured or in trouble, send me this stone in the mouth of your hunting-dragon, and I will come and rescue you.*'

Humungous gave a half-laugh, half-cry, as he looked first at the heart's stone, and then down at Toothless, collapsed on the deck in exhaustion.

Isn't Fate artistic?

But what this all meant was that Hiccup was in trouble up there on the mountain, and that Hiccup had never in his life been more in need of his Bardiguard.

Humungously Hotshot the Hero pulled the bracelet on to his own left arm.

He leapt on to the back of his White Dragon, drawing his sword and shouting, 'Come on, Windwalker! Hiccup needs us! This IS our fight! TO THE VOLCANO!'

'Oh, b-b-brother,' moaned Toothless, sprawled on the deck, 'we aren't going up again, are we?'

The Windwalker swallowed hard, and picked Toothless up in its mouth, and took off up to the Volcano after Humungously Hotshot.

16. I DIDN'T MEAN TO COME HERE

'AT LAST!' gloated Alvin the Treacherous, smiling down at the petrified Hiccup.

'Now, see where your precious Heroism has got you. DEAD before you even get your first chest hair. Where is the Fire-Stone, before you die?'

Hiccup looked straight up into Alvin the Treacherous's murderous, scarred face.

Now that he knew he was about to die he wasn't scared at all, and he wasn't going to give Alvin the satisfaction of thinking that he was frightened.

Hiccup began to sing.

And for some reason the first song that came into his head was that ridiculous song that was one of Stoick's favourites, which just happened to be the lullaby that Hiccup's mother Valhallarama used to sing to him as a baby, when she was rocking him to sleep, snuggled up to her armoured breastplate.

It was a song that was said to have been made up by Great Hairybottom himself, many, many centuries before, when he first settled in the Archipelago.

'I didn't mean to come here…
And I didn't mean to stay…
It's just where the sea wind blew me
One acci-dental day…'

Alvin nearly dropped Hiccup, he was so surprised.

Alvin expected a person facing death to beg, cry, plead for mercy.

He didn't expect them to start singing songs as if they were casually sitting around a campfire.

'... I was on my way to America
But I took a left turn at the Pole
And I lost my shoe in a rainy bog
Where my heart got stuck in the hole...'

Above them the thunderclouds were so dark they were almost blue, and lightning crackled between them. Below them the Volcano rumbled ominously in reply. It was almost as if the small boy's voice was trying to placate the storm from above and the storm from below.

'What are you doing?' hissed Alvin in baffled and furious astonishment, his arm holding the Stormblade hesitating above his head. 'What ARE you babbling about? You're about to DIE here, you fool...'

Beyond Alvin's shoulder, Camicazi and Fishlegs, pinned under the swords of the Exterminator, joined in the song:

'*... I've heard that the sky in America*
Is a blue that you wouldn't believe
But my ship hit a rock on these boggy shores
And now I'll ne-ver leave...'

Alvin began to bring the Stormblade down, furious that Hiccup was going to die while apparently happily singing and enjoying himself, rather than afraid and alone, and as his arm carrying the wickedly sharp Stormblade swung down...

... ZZZZZZZZING!!!!!!

… out of the billowing mustard-yellow smoke belching from the Volcano behind Alvin's shoulder a white feathered arrow came singing, straight and true, towards Alvin's upper arm. The white-feathered arrow sank deeply into the weak human flesh of his bicep, and he dropped Hiccup on to the ground with a cry of agony.

The pure, clear noise of the young Vikings' singing rose up and cut through the thunder.

And then another voice joined in.

A much deeper, rather painfully LOUD voice, WILDLY out of tune, and yodelling and zigzagging up and down the scale like a gigantic crow having a fit.

"I DIDN'T MEAN TO COME HE-ERE...
AND I DIDN'T MEAN TO STA-A-AY...
BUT I LOST MY HEART TO THESE RAINY BOGS AND I'LL NE-E-E-VER GO AW-A-AY!!"

Oh dear, thought Hiccup in surprise, *something terrible really did happen to Humungous's voice when he was in the Lava-Lout Jail-Forges...*

That sounds terrible!

Through the smoke of the Volcano, Humungously Hotshot the Hero came riding.

He sat up straight and tall on the back of the White Dragon, putting away his bow now, and drawing his swords.

On his left arm he was wearing Alvin's bracelet, snaking brightly around his arm.

'Arm yourself, Alvin, you TREACHEROUS SNAKE!' shouted Humungously Hotshot.

Alvin whipped his head around to see Humungous riding straight for him. His great swords the Fireflash and the Mooncut held sternly above his head.

Alvin started in horrified surprise and yelled out 'EXTERMINATOR!'

The dreadful dragon heaved his claws out of the ground around Camicazi and Fishlegs, and came bounding towards his Master.

Alvin leant down, and dragged the arrow out of his arm with his teeth.

It was not, unfortunately, a deep wound, and although it bled quite a bit, it did not stop Alvin leaping aboard his Exterminator's back, and up into the air.

And in the swirling smoke of the Volcano, the two Warriors faced each other for the first time. Alvin pulled down the visor on his Fire-Suit. The dragons, one white, one black, wheeled around each other through the sulphurous smoke, watching for an opening, waiting for a moment to attack.

'Now, now, Humungous,' Alvin wheedled. 'Don't forget, I'm your old pal, Terrific Al. You wouldn't hurt an old friend like me, would you?'

But Humungous was full of righteous wrath.

'Friend? HA! You never delivered my ruby heart's stone! You kept it for yourself!'

A ray of sun poking for a moment through the rain-laden clouds bounced accusingly off the ruby in the bracelet, which was now round Humungous's arm.

Both men let out a terrible scream, simultaneously, and they leapt together, the two Warriors' swords meeting with an awful clang of metal against metal, Stormblade against Fireslash.

At exactly the same moment, there was a great CRASH of thunder, the heavens opened and it began to POUR with rain.

Fishlegs and Camicazi ran towards Hiccup, and all three Vikings huddled together straining to see what was happening up in the sky, who was winning the Battle in the Smoke.

The Windwalker appeared out of nowhere, and dropped Toothless on to the top of Hiccup's helmet. Toothless looked into Hiccup's eyes upside-down, exhausted but thoroughly overexcited.

'L-l-look, I brought H-H-Humungous, Toothless saved the day, Toothless a Hero, Toothless a Hero!' chanted the little dragon jubilantly, letting out a gloating cock-a-doodle-doo of triumph.

'GUYS!' yelled down Humungous, performing the Grapple-lunge with full twist, as he fought all ten of the Exterminator's sword-claws AND the Stormblade and Alvin's hook on top, 'DON'T FORGET THE QUEST!'

(This may seem like rather obvious advice, but trust me, in the heat of the moment it is quite easy to forget what you came for in the first place.)

'YOU'VE GOT TO GET THE FIRE-STONE IN THAT VOLCANO *NOW*, OR WE'RE ALL DONE FOR!'

'Yes, well done, Toothless, but we're not safe *yet*,' said Hiccup shakily, trying to find where Camicazi had left her waistcoat, but it was difficult to see in this driving downpour. 'We have to throw the Fire-Stone in the Volcano...'

'I think I put it somewhere over there...' said Camicazi, uncertainly, pointing vaguely to the right, '... or was it somewhere else... I can't quite remember... I mean honestly you put something down for *one* moment and...'

'N-n-no you're right!' screeched Toothless, wild with excitement, 'Toothless get the Fire-Stone n-now... Toothless be the H-H-Hero for once!'

'No, Toothless, hang on,' said Hiccup, clinging on to one of

206

Toothless's legs. *'We'll do it, Toothless, don't worry, we'll do it.'*

But the glory of Humungously Hotshot telling him what a great Hero he was had gone quite to Toothless's head.

'Hiccup not t-t-trust Toothless, that's it, isn't it?' squeaked Toothless huffily. *'Toothless s-s-save Hiccup's life and still HICCUP want to be the big Hero all to himself... Well Toothless a Hero now too... and Toothless can do it ALL ON HIS OWN, j-j-just you see...'*

Toothless leant down, and gave Hiccup a painful little nip on the knuckle, so that Hiccup let go of his leg with a sharp cry, and Toothless spread out his wings and soared through the rain, with Hiccup running after him shouting:

'No! Toothless! Wait!'

But Toothless didn't quite catch the last bit because he was searching the ground for the Fire-Stone.

Toothless can do this all on his OWN

'It's here somewhere... s-s-somewhere... Aha!'

The little dragon spotted the already sodden waistcoat with a gleam of gold in it lying sitting in what was now mud, not very far away, and he swooped up to it, claws outstretched.

C-C-C-C-C-CRASHHHHHH!!!!!!!!!

A great crack of lightning skewered through the black sky above.

A tremendous rumble of *something*, it could have been thunder, it could have been the Volcano...

'GUYS!!' shouted down Humungous, swooping down on a cringing Alvin, and performing the Grimbeard's Grapple, the Piercing Point, the Half-turn Demi-Plunge, and the Deadly Double-Act, four entirely different and immensely difficult sword-plays in quick succession.

'*WHAT ARE YOU DOING DOWN THERE?*

Oooh it's a bit h-h-heavy.

YOU REALLY,
REALLY NEED TO
GET A MOVE ON!'

Toothless
unwrapped the
Fire-Stone from the
waistcoat and took a
good hold of it.

He looked over
his shoulder.

*Toothless
can DO IT,
T-T-Toothless
can DO IT*

Hiccup, Fishlegs and
Camicazi were running down the mountainside
towards him through the driving rain, Hiccup still calling
out: 'NO! TOOTHLESS! I'LL DO IT! IT'LL BE~'

Toothless gave a defiant little snort and a toss of
his head.

'Toothless d-d-do it on his OWN,' he said, and
lifted the Fire-Stone up in his claws.

But the smooth, golden surface of the Fire-Stone
had become slick and slimy in the driving rain. And
Toothless's sharp, pointy little claws didn't have the grip
on it that they might have done when it was dry.

'~SLIPPERY,' groaned Hiccup.

Hiccup, Camicazi and Fishlegs reached the

waistcoat just in time to get an excellent view of the Fire-Stone sliding from Toothless's clutching talons and beginning to roll down the mountainside that they had so painfully, so slowly, so bravely come up.

'Whoops!' squeaked Toothless guiltily. 'S-s-sorry... what a butter-claws I am... Don't worry... don't panic... m-m-me get it...'

And he made another dive for it, getting in the way of Camicazi, who was just trying to tackle it from the other direction.

'Got it!' cried Camicazi, in a split second of triumph, before Toothless crashed into her face, and knocked the muddy golden Stone out of her fingers.

'Whose side are you *on*, Toothless?' howled Hiccup, as he passed Camicazi and Toothless sprawled in the mud, and pelted after the rolling Stone, now gathering speed and bouncing merrily down the steep slope through the soaking, drenching, drowning rain, lightning crashing all around it.

On and on it rolled, and with every foot that it bounced, the success of their Quest was rolling further and further away from them.

Up in the air, despite being mounted on a far superior dragon, Alvin the Treacherous was being

W-W-WHOOPS!

THOROUGHLY beaten in the sword-fight by
Humungously Hotshot the Hero.

Humungous had already thrust his spear into
one of the Exterminator's hearts, and although the
Creature could still fly because it still had the other
heart to keep it going, some of the fight had gone out of
it. Can you blame it?

Alvin was preparing to desert, for if ever a person
knew how to run away when things looked bleak, it was
Alvin the Treacherous.

But Alvin looked down, and he saw the golden
globe rolling down the mountain, with the three little
figures and their dragon scrambling, sliding, and falling
after it.

Alvin saw a chance to snatch Victory from the
jaws of Defeat.

To Humungous's surprise Alvin stopped
the Exterminator mid-charge (this was
most certainly NOT considered good
Barbarian Behaviour, running out
on a fight) and wheeled his
dragon round, and swooped
after the rolling, fleeing
figures and the Stone.

The ground was flattening out a bit, and the Stone slowed a little before colliding with a large rock and coming to an abrupt stop.

The Windwalker got to it first, and looked nervously up at Hiccup, waiting for instructions.

'It's stopped!' called out Camicazi in relief to the others, as she struggled and slipped downwards. *We can get it now...* thought Camicazi.

We can get it now...

We can get it now...

Three sets of fingers reached out for the Stone, and...

'*TOO LATE!*' crowed Alvin, swooping down on his Exterminator, and reaching down with his Fire-Suit-gloved hand, he picked up the Fire-Stone and bore it upward, up and up as fast as he could in triumph.

'You are TOO LATE. You will never stop the Volcano now.'

They *were* too late.

The Exterminator was swift of wing, even with a spear stuck in one of its hearts, and it soared up quicker than the White Dragon could follow.

The Volcano gave an angry hiss and a snarl, and then a furious warning belch, in a truly gigantic rumble

214

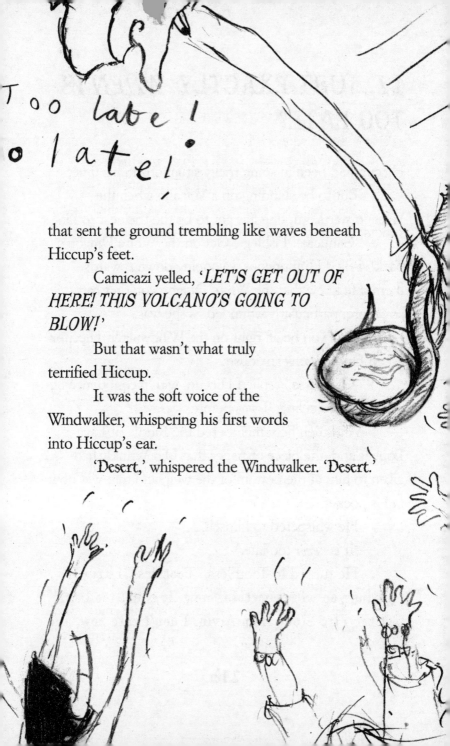

Too late!
o late!

that sent the ground trembling like waves beneath Hiccup's feet.

Camicazi yelled, '*LET'S GET OUT OF HERE! THIS VOLCANO'S GOING TO BLOW!*'

But that wasn't what truly terrified Hiccup.

It was the soft voice of the Windwalker, whispering his first words into Hiccup's ear.

'Desert,' whispered the Windwalker. 'Desert.'

17. JUST EXACTLY *WHEN* IS TOO LATE?

Hiccup had been in some tricky situations in his time.

But to be standing on a Volcano when the Volcano starts erupting has got to be the trickiest so far.

'Camicazi! Fishlegs! Get on the White Dragon's back!' yelled Humungous, swooping down towards them. He knew that the White Dragon couldn't carry any more, particularly wounded as she was.

'Will you be all right on the Windwalker, Hiccup?' asked Humungous anxiously.

'Of course,' replied Hiccup, with a confidence he was far from feeling. 'I was before, wasn't I?'

And then he remembered the Riddle of Lava-Lout Island, the piece of paper that Old Wrinkly had given to him at the bottom of the well, and that was now in his pocket.

He whispered to himself.

'It is *never* too late.'

He turned to Toothless. 'Toothless, I am trusting you with something now. It is not too late. Get the Fire-Stone from Alvin, I don't care how, and

throw it into the Volcano anyway. EVEN IF
THE VOLCANO HAS EXPLODED ALREADY,
Toothless, THIS IS VERY IMPORTANT.'

And Hiccup climbed on to the Windwalker's
back and the Windwalker began to run down the
mountain.

The poor wounded White Dragon struggled
to lift off carrying the three Vikings. But on the third
attempt she achieved it, and fumbled into the air.

Fishlegs had his eyes absolutely tight shut.
This was his first flying experience, and it had to be
said it was one that wasn't likely to make him feel
confident about flying. I think you would describe it as
TURBULENT. The White Dragon would flap forward
for a couple of moments and then drop like a stone for
twenty metres, leaving Fishlegs's stomach some way
behind.

'We're going to die…' whimpered Fishlegs, as
they plunged down towards the little sail of *The Peregrine
Falcon* in the bay, which had now been joined by the
sails of Stoick and Big-Boobied Bertha's boats.

'Oh stop moaning,' snapped Camicazi. 'I'm
much more worried about Hiccup.' For at least
the White Dragon was FLYING, in a fashion. The

Windwalker's wings weren't strong enough yet to take off with Hiccup aboard. Camicazi was peering at the tiny figure of the Windwalker running down the mountain.

Hiccup clung to the Windwalker's skinny neck.

'Run,' he whispered. 'Please, run, run, run.'

'R-r-r-r-run!' squeaked Toothless, flapping furiously after Alvin. 'Run, run, r-r-run!'

BOOOMMMMM!!!!!

The Volcano exploded.

18. HERE'S AN INTERESTING QUESTION. CAN YOU OUTRUN AN EXPLODING VOLCANO?

Here's an interesting question.

Can you outrun an exploding Volcano?

The answer is, if you survive the initial explosion, you *can*, depending on the type of lava.

Some lava runs extremely slowly. Some lava runs horribly quickly.

It depends, in short, on the Volcano in question.

And you can't really tell what kind of Volcano it *is* until the Volcano actually explodes.

When this particular Volcano exploded, the whole of the top half of the mountain blew right off. A great mushroom of cloud ballooned up into the air and rolled out across the clear blue sky. The entire island vibrated, churning up the seas round about and sending *The Peregrine Falcon*, *The Blue Whale* and *The Mighty Momma* rocketing up and down the gigantic waves, and sending the hearts of the two parents aboard those ships plunging up and down with it.

Great chunks of burning mountain were blasted up into the air and rained down to the ground and into the sea. The Windwalker screeched to a halt as a truly gigantic flaming boulder that could have squashed them flatter than two pieces of paper crashed to earth right in front of them, close enough to graze the Windwalker's quivering nostrils.

The Windwalker leapt on, dodging the flaming rocks falling out of the sky, and now running over the Exterminator Eggs that stretched before him in a great carpet all the way down to the sea.

Hiccup looked over his shoulder.

Burning rivers of hot molten lava were shooting out of the top of the crater and racing down the sides of the mountain.

It really wasn't Hiccup's lucky day.
Depending, of course, on the way you look at these things, whether you are a 'glass half full, or glass half empty' kind of person. You COULD, for instance, say that Hiccup had been really rather lucky to survive the day so far.

It turned out, as bad luck would have it, that the lava on Lava-Lout Island was the extremely fast-running kind that races in a red-hot river of death at speeds of over seventy miles per hour, much, much faster than a man can run – but was it faster than a Windwalker? It already seemed to be catching up with them.

'R-R-R-R-R-R-RUNNNNNNN!!!!!!!' screeched Hiccup again, as if the poor Windwalker needed telling, already running as fast as he possibly could, ears back, smoke steaming from his nostrils, taking great gasping breaths as he rocked forward in his extraordinary, limping run.

The lava streams shot down the mountain, horrible, steaming bright-red rivers.

And it wasn't just the lava which was chasing them.

You'd have thought that things couldn't get any worse – but things can always always get worse.

The Exterminator Eggs were HATCHING the instant the lava touched them.

So that out of the red-hot streams came bursting thousands and thousands and thousands of Exterminator fledgelings.

You might have thought that these newborn creatures would be still sleepy, still shaky, after lying curled up in those Eggs for nearly two hundred years, but no, it was as if their long gestation had been driving them MAD, so eager were these animals to be off and killing, even in their first few seconds of life.

They burst out of the lava streams still curled up like fiery Catherine wheels, and unfurled themselves mid-air in a shower of sparks, shaking the lava from their unfolding wings.

And the first thing they saw as their carnivore eyelids snapped open, was ALVIN, hovering at the top of the exploding Volcano, holding the terrifying flame-gold Fire-Stone in his hand.

For the previous three months, they had been trapped in their Eggs, looking up at the great statues of Alvin scattered all over the island.

Now here was this familiar face in the flesh, aboard one of their own, screaming at the top of his voice 'AFTER THEM!!!!!' and pointing with his terrible copper-red sword at the shaking, terrified little figures of Hiccup and the Windwalker, fleeing from the lava streams like a fox from the Hunt.

The Exterminators didn't need much encouragement to obey. An ancient memory stirred in their tiny brains. They knew what THIS was.

This was PREY.

Ten sword-claws leapt from the ends of their fingers like flick-knives, and the Exterminator fledgelings took off in hot pursuit of the fleeing Viking and his dragon, shrieking as loudly as the Furies having their hair pulled.

Down shot the lava streams, rushing closer and closer, nearer and nearer, catching up with Hiccup.

224

Down, too, flew Alvin and the Exterminators, in their hundreds of thousands, like a gigantic cloud of homicidal bats.

Hiccup remembered what Humungous had said about Exterminators. They would attack *everything*, anything that moved, set fire to every blade of grass, every bush, every tree. There wouldn't be a single living thing for hundreds of miles in every direction.

Even if *they* survived (and at this particular moment, this seemed unlikely), the Quest itself had failed.

And they hadn't even saved the Archipelago after all.

The Volcano had erupted, and *nothing* could now put the Exterminators back into their Eggs. The genie was out of the bottle, the plague was unleashed, and the Archipelago would be turned to sooty ruin in a matter of weeks.

Great clouds of steam rose hissing up into the air as the pouring rain met the searing heat of the running lava.

'Don't fall over… don't fall over,' prayed a soaking wet Hiccup, racing down the mountain on the back of the Windwalker.

'D-d-don't panic! D-d-don't panic!' muttered Toothless, panicking like crazy, as he approached Alvin on the Exterminator from above. Alvin was helpfully holding the Fire-Stone high above his head, so that the fledgeling Exterminators would have a good view of it.

'H-H-Hiccup gave Toothless this j-j-job 'cos he t-t-trusts Toothless... Toothless NOT make mistake again,' said Toothless encouragingly to himself, praying that the Exterminator would not smell him through all this rain. 'Toothless gotta G-G-GRIP this time... GRIP...' and he practised gripping with his little talons, as he edged ever downward towards that tempting yellow Ball.

Toothless pounced just exactly as if he were catching a nice fat rabbit.

His claws closed around the Stone. They gripped... and held.

Alvin gave a shriek of horror as his hand closed on nothing.

He whirled around, but in the smoke, and rain, and thunder-and-lightning, he could not see what had attacked him.

His Treasure was gone.

Held firm, if Alvin could but have known it, in

the gripping claws of Toothless, as
he bravely swooped right into the
heart of the exploding Volcano…
and let it drop.

Down, down the beautiful
Stone dropped, like a golden fiery teardrop,
right into the seething bed of magma.

And Toothless flew up again, hiding in the smoke,
too terrified to come out for fear of the Exterminators.

Many pairs of unbelieving eyes were watching
the apocalyptic events unfolding above them. It was
like a scene from some great Cosmic Play. The great
thunderclouds crackling above. The rain pouring down
in drenching black drifts. The lightning spearing into the
exploding Volcano.

Camicazi, Fishlegs and Humungous watched
as they descended to the bay on the back of the White
Dragon.

Stoick watched, from the deck of *The Blue Whale*,
sailing, a little too late, to the rescue through the driving
downpour. He was close enough now to Lava-Lout
Island to just be able to make out a small black figure
fleeing from the lava streams on the back of a dragon
with a horribly familiar kind of limping run…

227

'That's not… Hiccup, is it?' he said uncertainly, squinting up at the Mountain. 'Please let that NOT be Hiccup…'

'I think it may be,' said a dripping Snotlout at his side, with a secret smile.

Hundreds and hundreds of Hooligans were watching from the Hooligan ships, and hundreds of Bog-Burglars too, for Big-Boobied Bertha had launched *The Big Momma* in search of her daughter.

'The lava is going to catch them,' groaned Fishlegs.

It was a dreadful sight, like being the audience at some primeval Hunt of the Gods, the tiny figures of Hiccup and the Windwalker fleeing like terrified foxes, and the lava streams and Alvin screaming behind them like some Dark Lord, and the shrieking Exterminators, getting closer and closer and closer.

The first racing, burning lava stream finally caught up with the Windwalker.

It did not hurt the Windwalker himself, for dragons' skins, as we all know, are fire-proof.

But a tiny, scorching red-hot speck of it just touched Hiccup's heel, and Hiccup let out a scream of pain that electrified the Windwalker, and it put on a turn of speed that it did not know it had, running as if its heart would burst.

But there was still nearly a quarter of the mountain to run down.

'That's it, I can't bear to look,' said Fishlegs, shutting his eyes.

'I'm going to stand up on your back, Windwalker,' whispered Hiccup.

And shakily, Hiccup got to his feet, upright on the back of the Windwalker.

'OK,' said Hiccup, looking over his shoulder, 'get ready for the impact...'

The lava stream came up underneath the Windwalker, and he breasted it like he was breasting a wave, his wings spread wide to keep him above the lava.

'Oh, for Thor's sake,' gasped Camicazi, 'you can look, Fishlegs, *look*, I've never seen anything like it, that's just INCREDIBLE...'

'BY THE BEARD AND ARMPIT HAIR OF THE GREAT GOD WODEN!' cried Stoick the Vast in astonishment.

'I don't believe it...' groaned Snotlout. 'How is he *doing* that?'

Hiccup Horrendous Haddock the Third, knees

bent, arms spread
wide, was SURFING
the lava streams.

   DOWN, he surfed
the red-hot lava, with the
Windwalker as his surfboard, just
exactly as he had surfed the waves of
the Long Beach on bits of old driftwood
as a child (but rather more expertly actually
– when the sea below you is boiling at seven
hundred and fifty degrees Celsius, it does tend to
concentrate a person's mind on keeping his balance).

   That final, impossible surf carried them the last
three hundred metres or so of mountain.

And then, *just* as they reached the edge of the sea-cliff, the Windwalker gave a great push and a LEAP with its hind legs to carry them forward so they didn't get caught up with the lava as it fell off the edge of the cliff.

Hiccup had made leaps such as these all his life. Leaps of faith, leaps of hope, leaps out into the unknown. Hiccup had always trusted in his luck, in his faith that the universe was ultimately kindly, a Good Egg, as Stoick would put it, rather than a Bad Egg, and would reach out and save him.

But this was more of a leap of despair.

The Windwalker leapt off the edge of the cliff, and his leap carried them *just* far enough to get out of the way of the lava – and then they plunged immediately downward. The Windwalker spread out its wings to break their fall, but its wings were not strong enough, and in a matter of seconds they had blown inside out like an umbrella in a high wind.

The Windwalker and Hiccup sank like stones to the sea below.

That plunge into the ice-cold sea was a terrible reminder that perhaps, just *perhaps*, the universe was not a Good Egg after all. They hit the sea at such a speed that it was like crashing into an icy wall. *Perhaps this is reality*, thought Hiccup as he sank below the waves. *This pitiless, uncaring, heart-stopping cold.*

And when he came spluttering up to the surface, gasping for breath, it was to the even colder reality of a great black cloud of Exterminators circling above them. A cloud that stretched right across the sky, blotting out the blue. A cloud that gave a shriek of evil joy when it saw their two little heads re-surfacing above the water.

'THERE HE IS!' shouted Alvin, his eyes lit up with savage joy, as he wheeled his Exterminator round for the final attack. 'GET HI-I-I-I-I-I-IM!'

The lava streams dripped off the edge of the cliff and dropped into the sea in an angry hiss of smoke. The black rain dropped steadily. The Exterminators pointed their beak-like heads downward, and dived in a great storm down towards the sea, their sword-claws held outstretched in front of them, ready to destroy.

So this is the end, thought Hiccup, as he watched them come down, the quenching cold turning his entire body numb. Nothing can possibly save us now.

BOOOOOOM!

The Volcano exploded for the second time.

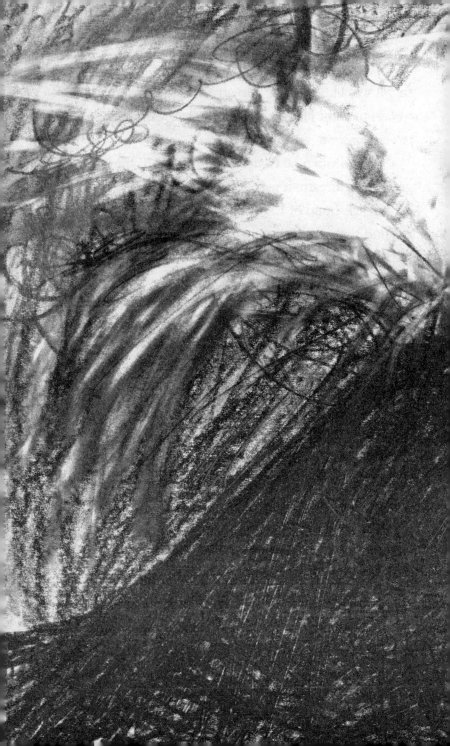

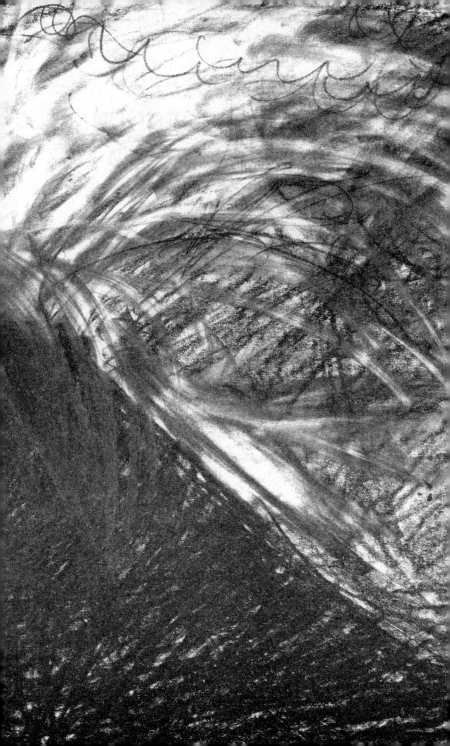

19. HERE'S ANOTHER INTERESTING QUESTION. IS THE UNIVERSE A GOOD EGG OR A BAD EGG?

The Exterminators paused mid-dive, as the sea, and the sky, and the islands themselves, rocked crazily round them.

This eruption was different from the first.

This time, what had happened was that the heat of the Volcano had HATCHED the Fire-Stone.

For one of the many secrets of the Fire-Stone, that Hiccup had worked out from Old Wrinkly's riddle (and I am sure that you clever readers and listeners have guessed this too) is that it is not, in fact, a Stone at all.

It is an Egg.

The Egg of the exceptionally rare Fire-Dragon. And one of the reasons that Fire-Dragons are so exceptionally rare is that the conditions required for them to hatch are so unlikely as to be virtually impossible.

For the Fire-Egg can only hatch in the heat and

turbulence of a Volcano that is exploding. But the Fire-Egg also gives out chemicals that PREVENT the Volcano from doing just that.

First, you have to imagine the extraordinary, impossible hugeness of a Fire-Dragon.

Then you have to imagine that hugeness all coiled up and packed inside an Egg no larger than a human head.

That is the Fire-Egg.

The walls of this Fire-Egg are made of a material so terribly, terribly strong that only a temperature of seven hundred and fifty degrees Celsius can melt them or crack them. Normally, the Fire-Egg is laid on a nook on the upper levels of a volcano crater, where the temperature never reaches levels high enough to hatch it.

But if it topples down (or in this case, is thrown) into the heart of the Volcano itself, and sinks down deep into the molten lava, then that kind of heat is sufficient to crack the unbelievably hard shell.

It takes about six or seven minutes, the same sort of time that it might take you to hard-boil a chicken's egg.

Then, when the shell is cracked, all that energy and hugeness packed down to such a pin-prick smallness is suddenly released in an instant and the Fire-Dragon EXPLODES outwards with an energy and a force impossible to describe, like a sort of mini Big Bang.

So what the Exterminators, and the Vikings, and Hiccup and Toothless saw was SOMETHING erupting out of the Volcano crater, SOMETHING that shot up so high it seemed as if it could touch the very stars.

Down on the deck of *The Blue Whale*, Stoick flung up an arm to shield himself from the brightness, for to look at it was a bit like looking at the sun itself, and pained the eyes.

'What *is* that?' breathed Stoick in awe.

Humungous and Camicazi and Fishlegs, who had landed safely on the deck of *The Peregrine Falcon*, forgot their fear as they gazed up in wonder at the extraordinary, terrible beauty of this sight.

The SOMETHING that erupted out of the Volcano was a DRAGON that seemed to be made entirely out of fire.

Of course, that is impossible, but this is what it looked like.

Gleaming muscles and scales of flame. Burning talons and scorching fangs.

It threw back its great fiery head and let out a

great ROAR that echoed across the islands, and even reached the trembling ears of the fleeing Viking Tribes miles and miles to the south, watching all this unfold on the horizon, standing silent on the decks of their rocking ships, soaked to the skin by the wildness of the storm.

The Fire-Dragon turned its great flaming red-gold eyes down towards the earth and they focused on the Exterminators, hanging below it in great black trembling clouds.

And when the Fire-Dragon looked at the Exterminators what it saw was PREY.

The Exterminators knew it too.

One minute *they* were the predators, leaping down towards Hiccup with greedy talons outstretched. The next, the world was shaking and vibrating around them, as if the gods had suddenly re-shaken the dice. And now that the world had stopped shaking again, *they* had suddenly become the victims.

The Vikings were now in the extraordinarily privileged position of being the audience to a scene played out in the blue skies above that had not taken place for hundreds and hundreds of years. A scene that dramatically demonstrated the exquisite balance of nature that Hiccup had placed such trust in.

The fight was played out against the background of the tempest at its peak, Thor's thunder rolling out magnificently from the blue-black clouds, great flashes of white sheet-lightning lighting up the drama in intermittent bursts, and then dying away to darkness.

Hiccup watched the combat lying floating on his back, in the grave coldness of the sea below, and the battle raging in the sky above him reminded Hiccup of a shoal of fish trapped in a tide-locked bay by a mighty shark.

The Exterminators shot shrieking across the surface of the stormy sky in their panic.

They scattered hither and thither, in great fleeing groups that sped across the firmament, splitting and re-forming as they dodged through the jaggedy lightning, right to the very edges and corners of the horizon

But however fast or far they flew, they couldn't escape the Fire-Dragon.

The Fire-Dragon never moved from its position on top of the Volcano.

It reached out with its great arms, flaming gloriously upward like tall watery trees of fire, and scooped up the Exterminators in huge handfuls, thrusting them down its glowing gullet with noisy relish.

It played with them like a cat does a mouse, letting them think they had got away, and then catching them up with its burning tongue.

The Fire-Dragon swallowed the whole lot of them, tossing them into his blazing mouth in their struggling thousands, plucking them out of their hiding-places in the smoke, sucking them in in satisfied, crackling bursts…

… until there was only one left, zigzagging across the sky like a demented blue bottle.

This was the one with Alvin on its back.

'You haven't seen the last of me, Hiccup Horrendous Haddock the Thi-I-I-ird!' yelled Alvin the Treacherous (but he was far too far away for Hiccup to hear him properly).

And then the Fire-Dragon picked up the Exterminator Alvin was riding by the spear in its breast, between two delicate flaming fingers, for all the world as if it were a wriggling worm on a cocktail stick... and down it went too.

The Vikings held their breaths.

Were they to be the next to go?

But no, the Fire-Dragon has *particularly* evolved to *only* feed on Exterminators.

The Fire-Dragon let out one final ROAR of triumph, the contented song of a meal caught and ready for digestion.

And then it leapt up into the sky, and dived back down into the Volcano crater, its great tail sending fresh waves of lava spilling over the top and down the sides of the mountain.

Swimming down, down, who knows where?

To the earth's core?

I can imagine it there in my mind's eye, swimming as free and joyous as a dolphin in those fiery waters.

There were two final flashes of thunder-and-lightning, louder than all the rest, whose rumbles echoed dramatically before growing gradually fainter and fainter...

And then all was majestically silent.

The peril was over.

The Volcano still spewed out its lava, but it was moving more slowly now.

The rain thinned down from deluge, to downpour, to drizzle, before petering out completely, to mere drips on the wind.

And even ALVIN, surely, *surely*, would find it difficult to swim his way up to safety through the burning waters of the earth's core?

The thunderstorm drifted away towards the Mainland, and the sun was coming out through the clouds. But the strange, boiling-hot weather had broken at last, and this was a very different sort of sun from the sun that had been beating down unrelentingly on the Archipelago for the past three months. This was a kindly benevolent sun, with a gently blowing cool breeze.

A great sigh of satisfaction went murmuring along the lines and lines of Vikings, watching from their boats to the south. One began to clap, and soon they were all applauding, as if what they had been watching had been some great Play.

'Bravo!' shouted out Mogadon the Meathead, stamping his feet on the deck of the ship, 'BRAVO!'

And the other Vikings followed his lead, cheering and clapping, and making ready to sail back to their homes again, their safe, quiet little homes in the bogs, that had been saved by this miracle.

'He's ALIVE!' cried Stoick the Vast, embracing the nearest thing to him, which happened to be his repellent nephew, Snotface Snotlout. 'He's ALIVE!'

'YES, I have this feeling that he probably is,' snarled Snotface Snotlout through gritted teeth. 'What excellent news.'

20. WHEN THE PLAY IS OVER

Camicazi, Humungously Hotshot and Fishlegs had
to sail *The Peregrine Falcon* across the Bay to pick up
Hiccup. By this time they had been joined by Stoick
in *The Blue Whale*, and Big-Boobied Bertha in *The Big
Momma*. The Windwalker flew across to them in order
to show them the way, because of course they couldn't
pick out one small lopsided helmet across those choppy
seas, that had been so stirred up by the explosions and
vibrations of the Volcano.

They were all extremely worried, because the
seas around Berk are very cold, and it is perfectly
possible to freeze to death if you spend too much time
in those icy waters.

But in fact Hiccup was all right. The red-hot lava
now pouring down from the cliffs had swiftly heated the
shallow waters of the bay to what was really almost a
very pleasant swimming temperature.

So he lay calmly on his back, waiting to be
rescued, letting himself float up and down supported on
the swell of the warm water, looking up into the blue sky
and thinking what a great joy it was to be alive.

Toothless had been hiding up in the great billows

of mustard-coloured Volcano smoke, peeking out
from his hiding-place in the drifts of cloud, absolutely
terrified.

But when he had satisfied himself that all the
Exterminators had been Exterminated, and the Fire-
Dragon meant him no harm, and had disappeared, he
sped like a whirring green butterfly down to the bay
where he was the first to find Hiccup, turning gentle
circles as he floated peacefully in the water.

'Toothless ∂-∂-∂rop the Stone in the Volcano!'
stammered Toothless, giving Hiccup a lovely surprise by
landing on his chin. 'All on HIS OWN.'

When Hiccup had recovered from the shock of the sudden arrival, and coughed out some of the sea-water, he stroked the little dragon's back, as Toothless licked his face with his little forked tongue.

'You,' said Hiccup, as the two of them revolved gently round, looking up at the sky, 'are a Great Hero, Toothless.'

Toothless lifted up his head and did his Victory Cock-a-doodle-doo.

And so when the others did finally haul him out, Hiccup was calm and relaxed.

'Are you hurt?' asked Stoick anxiously.

'No,' smiled Hiccup. 'I burnt my heel, but that's it.'

'THANK THOR!' bellowed Stoick. And then with a great roar of pride he enveloped Hiccup in a stifling hairy embrace. 'MY SON! I am sorry that I doubted you! We didn't let those Extermina-whosits beat us, did we? NO, by Woden and the lovely flowing armpits of Freya, we whopped their little Extermi-wotsit BOTTOMS, they never knew what hit them. THAT'S the spirit of the Horrendous Haddocks in you, NEVER SURRENDER! And by Thor's thighstrings we DID NOT. I can't wait to tell Valhallarama... Humungous, I have to admit, I owe you a great debt.'

He smiled, only a *trifle* reluctantly, at the irritatingly perfect Hero, sitting bloodstained but content on the deck. 'What a wonderful idea of mine it was to make you Hiccup's Bardiguard!'

Humungously Hotshot was looking happier than Hiccup had ever seen him before. A great weight had been lifted from his shoulders. He rolled up the helmet of his Fire-Suit, and ruffled his slightly-thinning-but-still-handsome golden hair.

'WELL, I'd forgotten what fun Questing could be, I really enjoyed myself there,' beamed Humungously Hotshot the Hero breezily. 'And I thought I didn't do too badly, considering I haven't done that sort of Hero Work for over fifteen years. A smidgeon out of practice, but not a bad effort, on the whole...'

'You were MARVELLOUS!' said Hiccup enthusiastically. 'STUPENDOUS! BRILLIANT!'

Stoick the Vast's smile froze behind his beard. But he had to admit that the guy had saved Hiccup's life. A Chief should give credit where credit was due, whatever his personal feelings. 'It was a fine piece of Bardiguarding, Humungous. You must name your price as your reward. Anything I have is yours, *anything at all*,

Humungous, you just have to say the word…'

'Well, it's terribly kind of you,' said Humungous. 'If you INSIST upon rewarding me, there is *one* thing I would like from you, Stoick…'

'Yes?' said Stoick.

'Your boat, *The Peregrine Falcon*,' replied Humungous. 'I plan to start a new life for myself, right here and now, and what I need is a good fast boat like this one so I can get away from here as quick as I can.'

'Are you quite sure?' asked Stoick. He had mixed feelings about this, because on the one hand, he was secretly rather relieved that this annoyingly brilliant Humungous wasn't going to be hanging round much longer, but on the other *The Peregrine Falcon* was far and away Stoick's favourite boat.

'I'm quite sure,' said Humungous firmly. 'If you're going to start a new life, you might as well start it NOW.'

Humungous smiled at Hiccup and patted him on the shoulder.

'Thank you, Hiccup,' said Humungously Hotshot, 'for finding my stone for me. It has meant a great deal to me in the past, but now I am looking to the future, and I would like you to have it.'

He leant over, and pulled the bracelet with the ruby heart's stone in it off his arm and gave it to Hiccup.

'I'm back in the Hero Business!' he said, happily swinging his sword from side to side, juggling it with his axe, balancing it on one finger, and then thrusting it back in its scabbard again. 'I'd forgotten how good it feels!'

Humungous took a big deep breath of the fresh sea air.

'I must say,' said Humungous, 'it's a great day to start a new life.'

Humungous called across the waves between the two boats, and he was so far away now that Hiccup could only just catch the words.

'Send my regards to your mother, Hiccup!'

Hiccup shouted back to say that he would.

'And thank you for giving me back my gift!'

'Your gift?' Hiccup shouted back.

'The singing!' called Humungous. 'It's such a pleasure to be making music again!'

And then Humungous began to sing.

It wasn't the song that Hiccup's mother used to sing to him as a child.

It was a new song.

Humungous threw out his chest and really gave that song some *welly*, at the top of his lungs, wildly out of tune and sounding like a couple of warthogs in a catfight.

"The Hero cares not for a WILD
Winter's STORM
For it CARRIES HIM SWIFT
ON THE BACK OF THE STORM
ALL MAY BE LOST AND
OUR HEARTS MAY BE WORN
BUT
A HERO FIGHTS FOREVER!"

Hiccup, Toothless, Camicazi, Fishlegs and the Windwalker had heard Humungous's novel way of singing before, and all five of them had stuffed their fingers or wings over their ears before he even started.

But this was new to Stoick the Vast.

His mouth flopped open for a few, astonished minutes.

And then a great grin spread across his face.

What a delightful surprise!

It seemed that even Humungously Hotshot couldn't be good at EVERYTHING.

'WELL,' said Stoick, rubbing his hands

251

together with satisfaction, 'I think we can do better than that, boys, can't we?'

'WE CERTAINLY CAN!' roared Gobber. And there were cries of 'YOU BETCHA!' and 'COULDN'T ANYBODY?' from Baggybum the Beerbelly and Nobber Nobrains.

'ALL TOGETHER NOW!' cried out Stoick.

And the whole Tribe put their hands on their chests, and sang their hearts out, all together, the words rolling out into the peaceful afternoon, in deep and gorgeous harmony:

'UP with your SWORD and STRIKE at the GALE,
RIDE the rough SEAS for those WAVES are your HOME
WIN-TERS MAY FREEZE but our HEARTS do not FAIL,
...HOOLIGAN..HEARTS.. FOREVER!!!'

And *The Blue Whale*, carrying Stoick, Fishlegs and Hiccup, Toothless, the Windwalker, and the Hooligan Warriors turned its nose towards the east.

Sailing along the rays of the sun towards the little Isle of Berk, a small, quiet, marshy little island that nobody notices much, but one on which there will be

Hooligans for as long as Great Hairybottom's shoe is buried in that bog.

Their song was echoed by that of the Bog-Burglar Warriors, sailing with Camicazi and Big-Boobied Bertha in *The Big Momma*, towards the Bog-Burglar lands to the south, getting fainter and fainter as they got further and further away from *The Blue Whale*:

'STRONG are the BREASTS that CRUSH WITHOUT FEAR,
MIGHTY the PLAITS that can STRANGLE the WIND,
NIM-BLE THE FINGERS that BUR-GLE the BOG,
...BOG-BURGLARS...STAND...TOGETHER!!!'

Hiccup did not join in the singing. He stood on the deck of *The Blue Whale*, Toothless asleep on his head, the Windwalker pressed to his side, watching as the tiny dot of *The Peregrine Falcon* got smaller and smaller,

253

travelling towards the WEST, towards new lands,
and new adventures, and feats of strength, and daring
Sagas that Hiccup felt sure that he would hear about
sometime in the Future.

And even when *The Peregrine Falcon* was so small
that it was a tiny moving speck on the horizon, Hiccup
still fancied that he could hear the faint, out-of-tune
noise of Humungous's singing.

'THE HERO CARES NOT FOR A WILD WINTER'S STORM
FOR IT CARRIES HIM SWIFT ON THE BACK OF THE WAVE
ALL MAY BE LOST AND OUR HEARTS MAY BE WORN...
BUT...
A HERO... FIGHTS... FOR-EVER!'

Humungously Hotshot was back in the Hero Business.

THE OLD MAN IN THE HOLE

Some hours later, an old man was sitting in a hole of his own making.

He had heard the sounds of the Volcano exploding far in the distance, and a distant thunderstorm, but of course he could not see what was happening.

He sat in the darkness, praying that it would all be all right.

Please, let it be all right... Please, let it be all right... Please, let it all be all right...

For hours he sat quietly.

And then to his relief the heads of a smiling man and a smiling boy appeared in that circle of blue.

The boy said: 'You can come up now, Grandpa. I told you that I would make it all right.'

'I knew you would,' said the old man, at last able to speak. 'At least... I think I did...'

And the boy helped him up the ladder and into the light.

EPILOGUE BY HICCUP HORRENDOUS HADDOCK III, THE LAST OF THE GREAT VIKING HEROES

Human hearts are not made out of stone.

Thank Thor.

They can break, and heal, and beat again.

I never spoke to my mother about Humungously Hotshot, and she never once mentioned his name.

I watched her very closely when she returned from her Quest, and my father was bustling all around her, chatting excitedly all about the Volcano, and how the Barbaric Archipelago was nearly wiped off the planet by 'those wretched Extermi-thingummys, *you'd* have given them what for, Vally my darling, oh my goodness, we could have done with *your* help, but we remembered what you always say, *Never Surrender*! And we didn't, did we, Hiccup?'

When my father got to the bit about how Humungous the Hero had appeared out of nowhere after all those years when everybody thought he was dead, just at *exactly* the right moment to save the life of her only son, my mother bent down very quickly to adjust the leg straps on her armour.

She was down there for quite a while, adjusting those leg straps, but when she straightened up again, her face, though a little red, was perfectly calm, and she smiled at my father, and kissed him on the cheek, and she said, 'You are quite right, Stoick, my dear. Never surrender. Shall we go in for dinner?'

Who knows what she felt, that long, long time ago, when Humungous first failed to come back from his Quest. Whether she, too, used to watch from her window, out to the sea, yearning and yearning, waiting and waiting for him to come sailing back to her.

And he never came.

Many many years later, when I was a tall grown-up man, and my mother was an elderly woman, my mother was climbing on to her riding-dragon, getting ready to go off on yet another of her Quests, and this was a bit trickier for her now because despite being a grandmother she still insisted on wearing full body armour.

She wobbled on to the dragon's back, creaking horribly at the joints, with two poor Warriors trying to assist her, and with her snapping at them, 'I don't *need* your help, I am *perfectly* capable of climbing up here on my own,'

Did I dream it or, as she swung unsteadily upwards, did something really come loose from around her neck, and drop for a moment into the sunlight? Did it catch a sun-ray, and wink at me, one small red wink?

I *think* I saw the ruby heart's stone, hanging around her neck on a fine golden chain.

It was only for a second, that wink of her heart that she normally kept so guarded, because as soon as she got herself settled on the dragon, she picked up whatever-it-was, and stuffed it back inside her armour again.

Then she pulled down her visor, so that her lined, old-woman face disappeared, and all you could see peering out was her eyes. Time had not aged those eyes, they were the same bright blue that once gazed out at Humungous all those many years ago.

'Yoicks!' my mother cried out in youthful excitement, anticipating the fun of the Quest ahead, and she kicked her dragon's flanks with her heels, and flew off into the heavens.

I watched her go, a tall armoured figure sitting upright on her dragon, her white hair flowing out from under her helmet, her sword still steady in her hand, getting smaller and smaller until she disappeared into the clouds entirely, and all I could hear carried to me on the wind was the last echoes of her voice crying out:

'Into the Battle!'

I never saw her again.

She was killed on the battlefield that very afternoon, seventy-six years old, and still fighting.

She was a Great Hero, my mother.

THE BRACELET

I set my mother's half of the ruby heart's stone in the other eye of the dragon on the bracelet. So now both halves of the stone are together again.

I did wonder whether I should wear something that had been worn so long by Alvin himself.

But then I thought, *my* fate and *Alvin's* fate have been so entwined round each other, in an endless tangled knot, that it is impossible to pick them apart.

If Alvin had not stolen Humungous's heart's stone, the hearts of Valhallarama and Humungous would never have been broken.

My mother would never have married my father.

And I, the hiccup, the accident, WOULD NEVER HAVE BEEN BORN.

And, by a curious, unexpected turn of Fate, I, Hiccup, also just happen to be Alvin's nemesis. So that all that Alvin's busy evildoing achieved was the accidental creation of his own downfall.

You see how good and evil are twisted together?

Like a golden dragon bracelet snaking brightly about a person's arm.

The dragon bracelet that Humungous created,

out of misplaced love and gratitude, in the hellish nightmare of the Lava-Lout Jail-Forges is exquisitely made, for he was a far better goldsmith than he was a singer.

It curls around my arm, its shining wings folded back, as if about to unfurl and take off, and now that its ruby eyes are set into the gold, you cannot see their tear shape, so they seem to be laughing rather than crying.

It is a constant reminder to me of the human ability to create something beautiful even when things are at their darkest.

I have worn that bracelet every day of my life.

Surely, SURELY, that was the last that we shall see of **Alvin the Treacherous?**

For surely even ALVIN couldn't swim back to life through the burning waters of the earth's core?

Or could he???

I have this funny feeling that we may yet be seeing more of this undefeatable villain...

Watch out for the next volume of Hiccup's memoirs...
A Hero's Guide to Deadly Dragons

This is Cressida, age 9, writing on the island.

Cressida Cowell grew up in London and on a small, uninhabited island off the west coast of Scotland where she spent her time writing stories, fishing for things to eat, and exploring the island looking for dragons. She was convinced that there were dragons living on the island, and has been fascinated by them ever since.

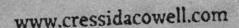

www.cressidacowell.com

HOWDEEDOODEETHERE!

For your latest news on all things dragon and Cressida Cowell please follow:

 @cressidacowellauthor

 @cressidacowell

 facebook.com/
cressidacowellauthor

Toodleoon for now...

'Cowell's How to Train Your Dragon
books are national treasures.'
Amanda Craig, *The Times*

'Bound to become a modern classic.'
Independent

'Always thrilling, funny and brilliantly
illustrated.' ***Daily Express***

'Cressida Cowell is a splendid story-teller
... young readers are lucky to have her.'
Books for Keeps

'One of the greatest inventions
of modern children's literature.'
Julia Eccleshare, LoverReading4kids

'Funny, outrageous and will lure in the
most reluctant reader.' ***Spectator***

'As with the best children's literature, these books
are about much bigger things: endurance,
loyalty, friendship and love.' ***Daily Telegraph***

'Cowell's loopy scattershot imagination is
as compelling as ever.' ***Financial Times***

CRESSIDA COWELL
HOW TO TRAIN YOUR
DRAGON

**ALSO AVAILABLE IN AUDIO
READ BY THE AWARD-WINNING ACTOR
DAVID TENNANT**

'If you have six to twelve-year-olds, and you don't know
about David Tennant's readings of Cressida Cowell's
How to Train Your Dragon series, you don't deserve to be
a parent ... Simply the best of kids' audio-listening,
and just as much fun for parents.'
The Times

'This kept us all laughing on the edge of our seats.'
Independent on Sunday

AUDIO
Read by
DAVID
TENNANT

Want to listen to an extract?
https://soundcloud.com/hachettekids

h
Hodder
Children's
Books